Murder
by
Misdirection

Debra Snow

MIND
BENDER
PRESS

Cover Design: Marianne Nowicki, PremadeEbookCoverShop.com
Editing: Brandi Aquino; www.editingdonewrite.com

ISBN-13: 978-1732659377
ISBN-10: 1-732659370

Published by:
Mindbender Press
474 South Main Street
Phillipsburg NJ 08865
www.mindbenderpress.com

Dedication

To my wonderful husband,
Arjay Lewis,
without whom this book would not exist.

"Magic is the only honest profession. A magician promises to deceive you and he does."

— *Karl Germain*

"Theft annoys me more than anything else. The purloining of effects from another magician. Some people think it's massive to steal the secrets of nuclear reactors, but to steal a card move is trivial. They're wrong."

—*Ricky Jay*

1. Indian Rope Trick

D etective Tom Chu sat in the driver's seat of his unmarked police car. Glancing in the rearview mirror, he moved his dark, straight hair off his forehead. He had narrow eyes that spoke of his Korean ancestry, and his slim fingers grasped the steering wheel. Since he was an expert in several forms of combat, he enjoyed the fact that he was thin and of average height. It always surprised a bigger man when his skills helped him take down a larger suspect.

He leaned his head back and closed his eyes, just as the sound of a finger ring tapping on his window caused him to raise his head and glance over.

"You takin' a nap?" the African-American woman at his window said, muffled by the closed glass.

Chu smiled, sat up, and hit the release to unlock the passenger door as his partner, Pro Thompson, came around the car. Chu reached over and opened her door as she carried two cups of coffee, the white paper emblazoned with the green Starbucks logo.

Pro got in, her gray pantsuit and white blouse giving her the look of a corporate professional. This not only hid her strong, fit body, but the shoulder holster and SIG Sauer P229 sidearm she wore.

Chu knew from his partner's workout regime that she could handle any situation a cop might face.

She handed him one cup and kept the other for herself. Chu took a sip; She prepared it just the way he liked it. That was the nice thing about having a partner: they knew your habits.

"So, were you sleeping?" Pro teased as she took a swig from her own cup.

"No, just enjoying the calm before the storm," Tom answered.

"What storm?" Pro frowned and looked out at the spring day. "There's not a cloud in the sky."

Chu looked over at his partner, her striking blue eyes in such contrast to her dark skin tone, which was the color of café au lait. "I mean the calm before our day gets busy."

"I heard that," Pro sighed and ran her free hand through her hair, which was short in the back and longer in front. It not only looked professional, but with the tight natural curl of her hair, it was a logical choice that required little care or upkeep. "But it might not get busy. We could just have a lovely spring day, sit in our car, and maybe even relax."

Tom smiled. "That would drive you crazy. You're an adrenaline junkie."

"Still, it could be a quiet day."

"Pro, we're homicide cops in New York City. Every day is crazy."

Pro looked out the windshield at the city—her city. They parked their car at a hydrant on the corner of 52nd and Ninth Avenue. She'd grown up only about thirty blocks north of here. She had to admit, the city never stopped, never slowed down, and she got a rush from being a part of it, being out there, making a difference.

Chu's cell phone rang with a very businesslike tone, and he reached under his suit jacket to pull it from his belt. "And so the craziness begins," he said, as he moved it to his ear. "Chu," he said as he hit the virtual button on his device. He looked to Pro, but she had already retrieved her detective notebook from her pocket and pulled out a pen. "258 West 47th Street? We're on our way."

Chu slipped the phone back into his belt and started the car all in one well-practiced move.

"We got a DB?" Pro asked, using the abbreviation for a "dead body."

"We do," Chu said as he glanced into the side mirror and slid the car into the busy traffic. "911 got a call. Uniforms got there fast. They have the DB and a suspect in custody."

Pro considered this. "That'll speed up the process. Seems like we caught an easy one."

"Yeah, it's good work when they catch the perp still at the scene," Chu agreed, as he weaved the car across several lanes to take a left turn down 46th Street.

Pro had pulled out the small rotating blue light and put it on the dashboard. Since they had a suspect in custody and traffic wasn't too bad, there was no need for sirens. As a New Yorker herself, she tried to avoid additional noise pollution in a city that was already far too loud.

They drove up 47th Street and pulled over to see an officer in front of a three-story brownstone. The uniformed man appeared younger than the mandatory twenty-one and gave the impression of a teenager playing dress-up.

The detectives came out of the car like a shot, and Pro smiled. She loved the fact that her partner moved as quickly as she did. He was the senior partner in the relationship, though he was only in his mid-thirties.

"Whaddaya got?" Chu requested as they moved toward the brownstone. Pro was happy to let her partner take the lead, though she could do so when needed. But her year of working with Tom Chu had taught her how to be a good detective fast. He would expect nothing less of her.

"Right here on the ground floor," the officer said, his Adam's apple bobbing up and down as he spoke. "Some kind of magic shop."

Pro broke into a smile. "Floss's Magic. I've been here."

Chu gave her a puzzled glance. "You have?"

"When I was a kid," Pro explained. "It's well known in the magic community. The guys who do that stuff hang out in the store all the time, usually showing each other card tricks."

Chu shrugged. "Let's see the scene."

The young officer escorted them up the short flight of stairs, and they took a left into a separate entrance next to the main door.

They passed through a door and into a storefront. There were glass display cases filled with flowers made from feathers and paper, and an enormous bouquet of what appeared to be fifty-dollar bills. Someone haphazardly repaired the cracked glass on several cases with nothing more than shipping tape.

Running up the walls on three sides were bookcases crammed with paraphernalia: there were wooden boxes with large, spotted dice resting on top of them; a small box of clear plastic filled with brightly colored silk handkerchieves; large coins of various currencies and holders to display them and possibly make them disappear.

However, the shelves had a layer of dust and all the tricks, though still impressive, looked old and dingy. The place was claustrophobic from the total amount of things that were packed in its limited space.

Standing near a red curtain to a back room was a female uniformed officer. She was average height, thin, with a strong, lithe body and short black hair under her hat. She stood at military rest, waiting for the detectives.

"Wow, this takes me back," Pro said, as her partner handed her a pair of rubber gloves. "It is exactly the same as it was twenty years ago."

"Really?" Chu said, as he pulled gloves onto his own hands. "I can't imagine you coming to a place like this."

Her mouth became a hard line. "I didn't choose it. I was a kid and brought to places like this all the time." She turned to the officer. "Tillie, isn't it?"

"Yes, ma'am." The officer smiled.

"Where's our vic?"

"Behind this counter," she told them, and stepped back so that Pro could get to the walkway Tillie had blocked with her body.

The pair of detectives looked over to see the man dead on the floor. He was older, with white hair and a pair of horn-rimmed glasses on his face. He wore cheap clothes that were worn at the elbows and knees.

"That's Albert Floss, the owner," Pro stated sadly.

"You know him?" Chu frowned.

""Yes, that case about a year ago? He was a magician at that magic club we busted."

"Right, Magic Over Manhattan. I remember," Chu replied, then turned to the uniformed officer. "Tillie, is forensics called in?"

"Yes, sir. They're coming from another scene. Going to be delayed."

"All right," Chu said and walked around the corner of the glass cabinet to crouch low near the body.

Pro leaned in. "Ligature around the neck," she noted.

Chu carefully opened the collar of the man's shirt to look at the line of red skin around his neck. He picked up a two-foot-long red rope that lay on top of the man's open vest. "Here's our murder weapon."

"Let me see," Pro said and took the end of the twisted braid in her hand. "No, this isn't it."

"Huh?" Chu replied. "It's a rope, and the marks suggest a rope was the murder weapon."

"Yes, but this is magicians soft-cut rope," Pro explained. "It would be much easier to strangle him with a real rope from a hardware store. This looks nice, but it's just foam rubber wrapped with a cloth tube."

"We'll let forensics figure it out," Chu said and rose. "Tillie, have you verified the ID?"

"Yes, sir, it's the owner, like Detective Thompson said," she replied

"Al Floss," Pro noted and shook her head as she stood. "He's been running this place for years."

"Anyone else work here?"

"Not from what I can tell, sir," Tillie answered and looked around the tight quarters. "And I doubt there would be room for two people."

"Where's the perp?"

"He's there in the back room, which is not much bigger than this one. My partner is watching him, and he's restrained."

"Good work, Tillie," Chu said. "Let's see him."

There was a battered, old red theater curtain in the doorway that possessed a faded glory. Tillie took the detectives to it and pulled it aside.

There was a male officer standing and a man in a chair with his hands fastened behind his back. The man had carefully coifed silver hair that had some black still mixed in at the top. On his face he had a mustache with a small beard, commonly called a "van dyke." With black pants, a black shirt with an open collar, and a beautiful black velvet sports coat, his outfit suggested a tuxedo. He raised his blue eyes to the detectives.

Pro gasped and Chu glanced at her, surprised by her reaction. The man slowly rose from the chair to his full height of six foot two. He brought his hands from behind his back as a pair of manacles clattered noisily to the ground behind him.

"Pumpkin!" the strange man stated joyfully. He opened his arms and took Pro into a bear hug.

This alarmed Chu enough that he released his service weapon from his holster.

"D-Dad?" Detective Pro Thompson stammered, as the two officers and her partner stared in disbelief.

2. Linking Rings

An hour later, while Chu tapped away at a keyboard, Pro stared through the one-way glass at her father in the interrogation room. "Did he get his phone call?"

Chu didn't look up but continued to type. "He even got two."

"Two?"

"Yeah, one was to his lawyer," Chu replied, and stopped to look up at his partner. "So, you want to tell me about this guy?"

"Not much to tell," Pro replied, still looking at the glass, her mouth a tight line.

"Oh, really?" Chu blurted. "He slips out of a pair of regulation handcuffs like taking off a bracelet. Then you call him 'Dad.' Next thing I know, he clams up, says he won't talk to anyone without his lawyer. At least we got him down here with no trouble. But you've hardly said two words since we picked him up."

"I was just surprised to see him," Pro fumed, still unable to look away. "His name is Maxwell Martin, but you probably know him as Max Marvell."

"That magician from television?" Chu frowned. "I thought he worked in Vegas."

"He did. I mean, he does. I mean, I don't know why he's here." Pro put her folded index finger to her lips in thought.

"You called him Dad. I always thought your dad was a cop. You told me your father passed away. What was it, two years ago?"

Pro turned to face her partner, and her eyes grew hard. "Joe Thompson was technically my stepfather. But to me, he was my father. He was a beat cop and an inspiration. He was the reason I went into law enforcement." She glanced back at the man in the closed room with anger. "This guy is just a mistake my mother made."

"Okay, I still need a little more information, Pro," Chu said, his hands open in a pleading gesture.

Pro sighed heavily. "Max and my mom were married, and I was born."

"That has been known to happen," Chu considered and tapped a couple of keys on his keyboard.

"Yeah, well, then he got hired for a huge show in Las Vegas. Pretty much just up and left us. I will give him the fact that he paid his child support and some extra, so my mother never had to struggle."

"A lot of men don't," Chu stated flatly as he looked from Pro to his screen and back.

She peered through the window where Max sat at the table. Gone was the velvet jacket, as well as his belt.

Chu could see moisture in her eyes as Pro spoke. "I worshipped him as a child, worshipped him like a fool. Then I visited him in Vegas a couple of times."

"I take it that didn't go well?"

"He remarried — to a racist bitch named Trixie, who had the IQ of a houseplant. She made it clear she didn't like Max's little brown mistake running around her house."

"Always wondered about your blue eyes," Chu said. "I used to think they were contacts."

"Genetic predisposition passed down… from our perp," she said and shook her head. "When we question him, I want in."

Chu finally stood. "I can't let you do that, Pro."

"I want to tell him what I think of him, and that if he killed that man—"

"You're too close, Pro," Chu interrupted.

Pro turned to her partner, her eyes aflame.

Chu spoke calmly. "Besides, he asked for a lawyer. I can't question him until the counselor arrives."

Pro nodded. "Okay, I won't ask him anything. Give me just two minutes to tell him off."

Chu exhaled heavily. "All right, but I'm observing you, and if you step out of line, you're outta there and off the case."

"Thanks, Tom," Pro said, and she walked to the door. Chu hit a button, a buzzer went off, and she stepped in.

The handsome older man looked up from the manacles which held him to the table. He didn't rise.

"Pumpkin!" he exclaimed, delighted as Pro walked in.

She leaned across the table from him and looked down at her father. "Don't you call me that. You have no right to call me that."

The bearded man smiled back amicably, the light dancing in his eyes. "It's what I called you when you were a kid. You loved it."

Pro sat. "I'm not a kid anymore, Max."

"Okay," he shrugged. "But here you are — a detective. It seemed like yesterday that you graduated from the police academy."

"Which you didn't attend," Pro fumed.

"I didn't want to be in the way. It was your day — yours and Joe's. I didn't want to come between you two."

"As I recall, you were also busy getting married to — which one was that? Mrs. Marvell number five, or was it six?"

"That was Judy," Max snorted. "Not one of my better choices."

"Sounds like she was the first one since Mom that didn't have a name like a stripper."

"I can't believe you are still angry over Trixie after all these years. I divorced her…"

"She was a freakin' redneck, Max!" Pro spat. "She hated my guts and let me know it."

"Well, I've always loved you."

"Unless you actually had to be a father."

"Prophecy—"

"Just Pro," she demanded. "Call me Pro."

"Your name is Prophecy," Max replied quietly.

"Another thing you hung around my neck before you took off and left me and Mom high and dry. You don't know all the trouble I had in school because of that name."

Max grew serious. "When you were a teenager, you made it pretty clear you didn't want to be around me."

"Damn straight. Joe was the man who really raised me, and that's why I took his name instead of yours."

"Well, I'm proud of you, if that means anything."

"Not a damn thing, Max." Pro rose and moved to the door and hit the intercom button. "I'm ready to leave."

The door buzzed, and without a look back, she stepped out into the hall.

Max lifted his freed arms and rubbed the wrists.

"Damn," Chu said out loud to himself from the window. "How the hell did he do that?"

Pro headed back to her desk only to hear her name called by a female voice. She turned to see the figure coming toward her. A woman about five foot nine, wearing a simple but fashionable dress that showed her slim figure nicely. Her makeup set off her salt-and-pepper hair and worked well with the tone of her dark skin.

"Mom?" Pro bleated in shock. "What are you doing here?"

Elisha Thompson approached her only daughter with a jacket under one arm and a purse in the other. "Your father called me."

"I see," Pro seethed and folded her arms. "You were his second phone call."

"He told me you arrested him," Elisha announced, and glanced around the busy bullpen.

Pro lowered her voice. "He was at a crime scene, and two officers found him with a possible murder weapon — a red rope — in his hands. We had to arrest him. He's a suspect."

"Oh, your father didn't murder anyone," her mother chided.

"Nice to see you, Mrs. Thompson," Chu said, coming over. "I haven't seen you since the Christmas party."

"Oh, thank you, Tom. And please, call me Elisha." She leaned her head back to stare down her nose at her daughter. "You've arrested Max?"

Chu could sense the tension between mother and daughter and moved closer to intercept. "We are holding him on suspicion of murder. It's pretty serious."

"Max refused to speak until his lawyer got here, Mom."

"You fingerprinted him and took a mug shot?" Elisha said with a frown.

"We had to, Elisha. It's protocol," Chu explained. "We are waiting for his lawyer, and then we are required to question him."

"If I could see him for a minute," Elisha suggested.

"Mom, I can't believe he dragged you down here," Pro said. "You should only see him through this window."

"What is that supposed to mean, Pro?"

Pro's mouth became a tight line. "Because you are always defending him. He twists you around his little finger—"

Elisha waved dismissively at her daughter. "You don't really think he did it, do you?"

"We can't be sure of anything until we question him," Chu explained calmly.

"Mother, we don't know Max. We don't know the man he's become."

"I know your father, Pro," Elisha said, rising to her full height. "He wouldn't harm anyone."

"Well, so far," Chu said, "he's released himself from two pairs of handcuffs. One at the scene and one here."

Elisha moved toward the window that looked upon her ex-husband. "Oh, he just does that to stay in practice. It means nothing."

"There you go," Pro snarled. "The great Max Marvell can do no wrong."

"It makes him a flight risk, Elisha," Chu said. "We take that pretty seriously."

"Let me speak to him, please," Elisha said.

Chu rubbed his forehead in annoyance. "I think we are going to have to reassign this case to detectives who are less involved."

"Please, Tom," she repeated.

Chu moved to the buzzer and gestured to the door.

"You're not going to let her?" Pro burst out.

"She's his ex-wife and the mother of his child," Chu considered with a shrug, then turned to Elisha. "But remember, I can hear everything you say."

He hit the buzzer and Elisha went in. Chu turned a dial on a small speaker and it crackled in response.

"Elisha!" Max said and rose from the chair. She opened her arms, and he took her in a hug.

"Seems like they still like each other," Chu observed.

"She always defended him," Pro grumbled, her arms folded. "Even after the way he ran off and all. She just loses any sense when she's with him."

The pair in the interrogation room separated, and Max held her at arm's length. "Look at you. You look great, as always."

"Thank you, sir," Elisha said, her face lighting up from the look in Max's eyes. She moved a hand to his temple and wove her fingers through the gray hair. "You finally stopped dying it. I like it. You look very distinguished."

Max shrugged. "More like extinguished. I am over sixty. I decided it was time."

"I keep forgetting how much older you are than me," Elisha said with a smirk.

"Not that much, young lady. But look at you. You've kept your figure, and I like what you've done with your hair. Here, sit, sit."

Max gestured to the chair across from where he'd been sitting as if he were meeting her for lunch instead of in a locked room in the middle of a police station.

"So, what are you doing here? Why were you with the man who died?"

"I can't talk about it until Mark gets here."

"You called Mark?" Elisha chuckled with delight. "I haven't seen him since our final divorce settlement. I always liked him."

"I didn't know who else to call."

"But you still haven't told me why you're in New York."

"To see you and Prophecy, of course."

"But what about your show?"

Max held up his hands. "It's closed. Elisha, I've retired."

The dark woman's mouth fell open. "Retired? You?"

Max leaned back in the chair and smiled at his ex-wife. "Vegas isn't what it used to be, and I've made more money than I ever thought I would, even with ex-wives and all."

Elisha clucked sympathetically. "I was sorry to hear about the break-up with Judy. She was always nice to me when we spoke on the phone."

Max leaned closer. "She was banging the pool guy."

Again, Elisha's mouth fell open in surprise and a laugh escaped her lips. She covered her mouth. "Oh, I'm sorry, Max."

"I'm not. Our prenup was ironclad. She barely left with the clothes on her back."

Elisha attempted to commiserate but couldn't stop herself from laughing instead.

Max sighed. "Face it, Elisha, I have lousy taste in women, except for you."

"Well, I never understood how you could go from me to Trixie. Honestly, what did you see in that girl?"

"She was quite flexible," Max suggested with a knowing wink. "It came in handy in the illusions and made some interesting experiences in bed."

This caused a fresh gale of laughter from Elisha. "That's what you get for thinking with the wrong head."

"Well, it didn't last five years, and she took me to the cleaners. It taught me to always have a solid prenup and to make sure I maintained ownership of my property and possessions."

"Who says an old dog can't learn new tricks?" she stated dreamily.

Max leaned forward and took Elisha's hand in both of his. "What tricks do you want to teach me?"

Her eyes half-closed, Elisha replied, "Oh, if memory serves me, the tricks you do are fine…just fine."

Pro knocked on the window, then hit the button on the intercom. "Mom, you need to come out!"

Max leaned back, the moment ruined. "The interrupting child! I am suddenly reminded why we didn't give Prophecy a younger sister or brother."

Elisha laughed again. "Well, I'll stay around until this is all settled, and then get you back to — where are you staying?"

"The Waldorf-Astoria. I might do some private shows, and that is always the best location."

"Retired, my ass." Elisha smirked and went to the door.

"Thanks for coming, 'Lisha."

"I wish it was under better circumstances," she said as the door buzzed and she went through it.

Back in the bullpen, Pro was standing with her hands on her hips and an angry look on her face, while Chu was on his desk phone.

"Honestly, Mother, get a room!"

"Don't start," Elisha warned.

"I can't believe you were in there making goo-goo eyes at that man," Pro whispered hoarsely.

"Your father. You can call him your father."

"Joe was my father. And I can't believe you could disrespect his memory like that."

Elisha sighed in frustration. "I loved Joe, and I was proud to be his wife. This has nothing to do with Joe."

"I was getting ready to get a fire hose to separate you two," Pro seethed.

"If you ask me, you could use someone in your life that would inspire a little fire now and then," Elisha shot back.

"Not today, Mother," Pro huffed.

"Then don't complain about me," Elisha sassed, keeping her voice low, "when the man who gave me my darling baby says a few nice things to me."

Pro surrendered. "All right, truce!"

A big voice called out, "As I live and breathe, Elisha Martin!"

Pro turned and Elisha looked past her daughter to see the heavyset man in the cheap suit as he walked toward them. He had a round face, and delight filled his eyes. He opened his arms to Elisha. "Elisha Martin—no, no wait, it's Elisha Thompson now, right?"

Elisha moved into the hug. "How are you, Mark?"

"Still practicing law. Someday I'll get it right," he laughed at his own joke. "Still married to Minerva, who loves me. God knows why. How is your marriage?"

"He gave me sixteen good years, but he passed away about two years ago."

Mark frowned. "Sorry to hear that. But look at you. Except for the gray in your hair, you look like you haven't aged a day." His eyes moved to Pro, and he grew serious. "Wait, can that be?"   H   e approached and looked carefully into Pro's blue eyes. "My goodness, Prophecy Martin, all grown up!"

"They do that, Mark," Elisha said.

Mark shook his head in amazement. "I guess so. You were the same age as my Jinny. I remember when you kids used to play together."

"Hello, Mister Jeffries," Pro conceded.

"Mister Jeffries? That's a long way from Uncle Mark!" Mark exclaimed and looked from one woman to another. "What are you two doing here? How did you know to come?"

Elisha spoke quietly. "Max called me, Mark. Pro was the arresting officer."

Mark turned to view Pro with new respect. "What, you're with NYPD? That's great! I don't really do criminal cases, so I don't see the police very often." He looked up at the taller Pro and chuckled. "So, little Prophecy Martin…"

Pro was having none of it. "It's Pro Thompson these days, counselor. Let me escort you to the suspect."

Mark glanced at Elisha, chagrined. "My, this is an unusual situation."

"Don't I know it?" Elisha responded sardonically.

3. Three Card Monte

Mark sat with Max in the interrogation room, and through the observation window Pro watched her father gesticulate while he told his story to the lawyer.

Of course, she would have loved to know what they were saying, but that would be in direct conflict with the lawyer/client privilege. So, all she could do was watch the silent show acted out in front of her.

"Are you all right?" Chu murmured, standing next to her. He glanced back to see Elisha sitting in the chair next to her daughter's desk, looking at her cell phone.

"Yes… no… I don't know," Pro conceded and shook her head. "It's like my entire past has come to hit me upside the head."

"Family drama and all that, huh?"

"Yes, but more than that. My parents broke up when I was five. And divorce turns any marriage into a business that's being dissolved. I mean, Max moved away, Mom met Joe, so all of their discussions about me, about money, were… businesslike."

"I guess that's how it is for most people," Chu agreed, and they both turned away from the window.

"Yeah, but today was different," Pro observed, looking over the bullpen, the movement of the detectives, men and women as they worked their cases. "For the first time, I actually saw my parents as people attracted to each other. That look in Max's eyes when he saw my mom. I never noticed that before."

There was a knock at the window, and Mark Jeffries was waving them in. Pro stepped forward, but Chu raised his arm to block her.

"Not you, Pro," he stated curtly.

"Tom, you can't do this to me—"

"I have to, Pro," he reasoned and turned to face his partner. "Look, that you were in on the arrest alone could give any lawyer reasonable cause to get this case dismissed. I can't have you in on the interrogation. You observe from out here."

Pro swallowed back her anger. "Yes, sir."

"When this is all blown over, you'll think about it and know I'm right, Pro."

"Yes, sir," Pro griped and stood by the button to buzz her partner in. Chu pushed the door open and stepped in as Pro turned the volume up on the speaker. She hit a button to activate the cameras in the room to record the interview.

Chu quickly stated his rank and the case number, then added, "Interview with suspect Maxwell Martin, aka Max Marvell."

This got a smile from Max.

"Mister Martin, you were discovered in Albert Floss's shop by two officers this morning at eleven hundred. Is that correct?"

Mark gave a nod to Max, who said, "Correct."

"They found you with what appeared to be a rope in your hand. Is that also correct?"

"Correct."

"Please explain why you were there with what appeared to be the murder weapon?"

This got a chuckle from Max.

Elisha moved from Pro's desk to stand next to her daughter.

In the interrogation room, Chu huffed, "Is something funny, Mister Martin?"

"Sorry. I found that rope on Mister Floss's chest when I arrived, and I picked it up out of curiosity. I found it funny, because that rope couldn't be the murder weapon. It wasn't even rope, but a special kind made for magicians from just foam with a cloth coating. You could no more strangle a man with that than you could climb a mountain with it."

Despite herself, Pro nodded in agreement and muttered, "Exactly as I thought."

"What was that, dear?" Elisha asked.

"Nothing, Mom," Pro replied, her eyes not moving from watching her father.

Chu leaned forward. "Could you please explain why you were there?"

"Certainly," Max declared. "I came to New York because Mister Floss was stealing one of my effects."

"Excuse me?" Chu challenged.

"He was stealing an effect of mine I named 'Prism.' It is an illusion I created for my stage show that uses two glass geometric shapes and the magician appears to vanish on a bare stage in a flash of rainbow light."

"Pretty neat," Chu mused, and made a note on a paper in front of him.

Max looked aghast. "Pretty neat? No, sawing a woman in half is 'pretty neat.' This is a routine that took me ten years to perfect. This one illusion redefines what is possible to accomplish live on stage."

Mark cleared his throat for attention. "Mister Martin owns the rights to the effect, and he protected it as a theater piece by the copyright laws of the United States."

"Seems like a pretty important trick to sell out of a rinky-dink magic shop, isn't it?" Chu pressed.

"He didn't have the equipment. He was trying to sell my method. I believe he had access to a full set of plans to recreate my illusion."

"You flew all the way to New York from Las Vegas because some guy figured out one of your tricks?" Chu questioned.

"No, a man who I thought was an old friend was stealing my creation. He was offering the plans to different people throughout the country. I wanted to talk to him, to tell him to stop. I was even willing to offer him money."

"So you got there, and what, got angry?"

Max sat up straighter in the chair. "Nothing of the kind. As I explained to my lawyer, when I arrived, Mister Floss was already dead."

"Really?"

"Quite! His door unlocked, and I went into the shop. I called for him and wandered around, thus discovering his body. The fake rope was on his chest. I reached down and picked it up at the same moment the police arrived."

Mark took over. "My client was just in the wrong place at the wrong time."

Chu's mouth grew tight. "Why couldn't he tell us this there and then?"

Mark and Max exchanged a quick glance, and Mark cleared his throat a second time. "My client had sent Mister Floss some, uh, rather unsavory emails."

Chu considered this. "Unsavory in what way?"

"Perhaps 'threatening' might be a better choice of words," Mark confided.

Chu shook his head. "I see. Does Mister Martin wish to add anything to his testimony?"

Mark looked at Max, who exhaled heavily. "I would like to know what he did with the plans for my illusion."

"Mister Martin, we are investigating a murder, not chasing down your trick," Chu told Max, then turned to Mark. "I will want your client to write up his account, and we are holding him until I get the report from forensics. If the timeline and the evidence agree with Mister Martin's account, I will speak to the DA about having him released."

"That could take hours!" Max whined.

"Up to forty-eight hours, Mister Martin. But that happens when you are found at a crime scene with a possible murder weapon in your hand. End interview."

Pro dutifully hit the button to end the recording of the session.

"See," Elisha said to her daughter. "Your father had nothing to do with that man's murder."

"Mom, Max's job is deceiving people. He could be lying right now," Pro said, as she pressed the button, which set off the buzzer as Chu and Mark Jeffries left the room.

"I can't believe you're saying that about your father."

"Albert Floss stole his big illusion? I have known people to kill for a lot less," Pro said, and headed to her desk. "Now you should leave, and I'll call you when we release Max — if he is released."

Elisha looked troubled. "I didn't know you still had so many resentments towards your father."

"Toward the man who abandoned me?" Pro said and turned to her computer, ignoring her mother. "Yeah, quite a few."

Chu was talking to Mark. "We have to keep him in holding until we get the forensic report and see what the DA says."

"I understand," Mark replied. "I'll contact the DA as well."

As they spoke, a uniformed officer opened the door from the outside and brought Max out, cuffing his hands behind him.

Chu turned to face Max. "Mister Martin, we are putting you in a holding cell by yourself. Please attempt no further escapes, or I'll lock you in your cell naked, like Houdini."

This made Max smile. "Detective, I am surprised you know Houdini did his prison escapes like that."

Chu didn't smile. "I've been partnering with a woman who knows a lot about magic and I finally know why. We can handle things much faster if you don't pull any tricks. Do we have an understanding?"

"Of course, detective."

Elisha rose. "Pro will call me when you're released, and I will come by for you, Max."

"Great," Max said as an officer led him out of the room. "Thanks, Pro."

Pro shook her head and looked at the report on the screen she had to fill out. "This is going to be a long day."

4. Passe-Passe

- -

Hours later, Pro and Tom returned to the precinct from another call they'd received—a robbery gone wrong at a bodega a few blocks away. The owner defended himself with his legal firearm, and the robber, a shaky drug addict with an illegal pistol, ended up dead.

"I guess it's better that the perp got shot instead of the owner," Pro sighed as she walked into the bullpen.

Chu nodded. "Uniforms confiscated the owner's firearm until we finalize all the evidence. It helps that he had a working camera pointed at the cash register."

"At least Mister Paulo could keep his business open," Pro said, referring to the owner by name. "This shook him up pretty bad. The last thing he needed was to be thrown into holding."

As they walked up the stairs, they saw a crowd around the processing desk where suspects went to turn in their belongings before being locked into holding. Pro and Chu heard laughter and applause.

"What the hell is going on?" Pro said as they approached.

"I don't know," Chu responded. "You find out. I'm going to get the report started."

Chu headed for the bullpen as Pro got closer. A circle of policemen and women had formed, and in the middle, taller than those around him, was Max. He wore his black velvet coat again and looked every bit the magician. He manipulated what appeared to be a large copper penny, only it was the size of a silver dollar. The collection of cops looked on in amazement.

"Of course, all you have to do is keep your eye on it," Max said as he appeared to grasp the coin with his right hand and hold it aloft. "No, I said watch it!" he chided, as he showed the right hand empty and the coin stood up at the tips of his left fingers.

"See, if you watch, you'll know it goes right here," Max explained, and he appeared to palm the coin as he placed it back into his left hand.

"No, it's in your right," a young woman in uniform said. She was a short African-American woman, who wore bright-red lipstick and worked traffic. She pointed at Max's right hand.

"See, you don't trust me," Max chuckled as he showed the right hand empty and opened his left fist to expose that the coin truly had been in there. He grabbed the shiny object with his right hand and held it out for the woman who had spoken. "You can look at it," he said and opened his hand, but the coin was gone.

This drew laughs from the crowd and one officer muttered, "Damn!"

"But it's actually right here behind my knee," Max pointed out, as he leaned forward to retrieve the coin from behind his leg. "It would help if it were bigger." With that, the dollar-sized coin was gone, instantly replaced by a much larger shiny coin the size of a beverage coaster. The large penny appeared to be far too big for him to even hold in his hands, and the assembled officers clapped and cheered.

Max bowed his head, held the large penny high, and said, "If I was truly a magician, I would vanish this!"

As if on command, there was a flash of fire in his hand and the coin disappeared.

"What's going on?" Pro bellowed over the noise and applause. "Why isn't my suspect in holding?"

The man behind the desk had been laughing along with everyone else. He became instantly serious. "Sorry, detective, word came down to release him. We returned him his possessions, and an officer recognized him from TV."

The woman officer drew close to Max and smiled. "I thought seeing you on television was amazing, but, wow, right here in front of us, I can't believe it." She pulled out a piece of paper that had a phone number scrawled on it. "I like what you do with your hands. Maybe you could give me a private show."

Max smiled a winning smile. "I would be delighted."

"Oh!" Pro snarled and moved between them. "Go back to your duties, officer. This man is old enough to be your grandfather."

With a sultry glance at Max, she moved away as he looked at the number in his hand.

Pro grabbed his arm and pulled him down the hall. "I can't believe you…"

"Hey, I'm single," Max defended.

They moved to a corner of the room as she hissed, "And you are embarrassing me."

"I saw no harm in entertaining the officers," Max responded. "And that girl — Trudy, her name badge said—"

Pro grabbed the paper from his hand, crumpled it, and threw it away. "For God's sake, you were making goo-goo eyes at Mom this morning—"

Max smiled. "Your mother is a fine-looking woman."

"And you are a bigger pig than I ever realized."

"She gave the number to me. I didn't ask for it," Max assured with a shrug. "Also, crumpling it up didn't help. You know I can memorize almost anything with one look."

Pro fumed. "If you phone that officer, I swear—"

Max put his hands up defensively. "I have no intention of calling her. You need to calm down."

"Calm down!" Pro shrieked, and then glanced about and lowered her voice to a whisper. "Since you showed up, you have turned my life upside down."

"I'm sorry, Prophecy."

"Pro!" she argued. "Call me Pro, dammit."

"Honey, they released me on my own recognizance, but I have to turn in my passport by tomorrow."

"Uncle Mark did his voodoo?"

"And the evidence backed up my story. But it's nice to hear you call him 'Uncle Mark.'"

"It was a slip of the tongue," Pro muttered.

"I'm just waiting for your mother. I promised to take her out to dinner."

Pro stopped dead. "What?"

"It's the least I can do for her having to leave her office and come over here," Max said breezily. "What's good in the area? It's been a long time since I was in New York."

Pro's mouth opened and closed like a fish, and she gave herself a quick shake. "This better not be a date."

Max beamed. "It's two old friends having dinner. Plus, as a responsible parent, I want to talk to your mother about the career path you've chosen."

Pro stared at him. "You want to…what?"

"Well, homicide," Max frowned. "I don't know if it's the best choice. I want to talk to your mother about some ideas I have that could fast track you to becoming a lieutenant. Did you know the mayor is an old friend of mine?"

Pro held up her hand and slowly balled it into a fist as she struggled to regain control. "Max, you need to stay out of my life."

"But, pumpkin—"

"Don't call me that," she spat. "And stay away from my mother! She's been vulnerable ever since Dad died, and I don't want you taking advantage of her."

"Stepdad," Max corrected.

"The dad that didn't mess up my life. How's that?" Pro announced triumphantly. "Now, they released you. Do me a favor and leave."

For a moment, Max's eyes appeared wet as he looked into her blue eyes the same shade as his own. "If that's what you want, Pro," he muttered sadly.

"Yes, that's what I want," she grunted. Then she turned, fully intending to walk away.

Coming down the hallway was a woman walking with a familiar gait. It took Pro a moment to realize it was her mother. She wasn't sure how she'd filled her day, but Pro realized she must have spent it getting a makeover. They set her hair in a new style, her makeup, something Elisha always prided herself on, was now flawless. She wore a black dress that hung on each curve as if someone had painted it on, and a black wrap with red roses embroidered on it lay on her shoulders.

Pro stopped, and her mouth fell open. She glanced back at Max to see him wearing the same open-mouthed expression. She noted that her mother's eyes never even went to her, but focused on Max like a laser.

Elisha strode past her daughter.

Pro noticed that the older woman had given up her comfortable shoes and was wearing heels that made her an even more imposing figure.

Max moved to her without hesitation. "My God, 'Lisha, you are astounding."

"Flatterer," she said as she took a quick spin to show off what had to be a new dress.

"No, I mean it. You looked great this morning, but now! I cannot find words to describe you."

"The mouth falling open did it for me. 'Bout time someone made you do that instead of the other way around," Elisha said, and for the first time noticed Pro. "Oh, hi, honey."

Pro did her fish impression a second time as she tried to wrap her brain around her mother's transformation. "Mom...?" she finally blurted.

"Shall we go?" Max said, taking her arm.

"We should. Remember Patsy's?"

Max looked at her with glee. "Do I ever!"

"It's still there, and I made us a reservation," Elisha suggested.

As they walked past Pro, her mother gave a wave and said, "See you later, honey."

Pro watched her parents as they headed for the stairs and shook her head in disbelief.

"They make a handsome couple," Tom Chu said, suddenly at her side.

Pro turned to him with fury in her eyes. "Don't go there," she groaned, as she made her way back to her desk.

5. Professor's Nightmare

E arly the next morning, with two cups of designer coffee in her hands, Pro got off the elevator near her mother's apartment. She had grown up in the simple West End Avenue abode and could recall playing up and down the hallways as a child.

When her mother married Joe, he had moved in with them and it had been just the three of them. Although it disappointed Elisha that her marriage to her second husband had been childless.

Joe threw himself into raising Pro like she was his own and adored her as she grew. He taught her self-discipline and knew how to be there when she needed someone to lean on, and to back away when she needed to spread her wings.

Pro stopped in front of the door, put the coffee cups on the floor, and unlocked the apartment with practiced ease. She picked up the cups and pushed the door closed with her hip as she walked in.

Bringing her mother coffee was a Saturday ritual they had held onto ever since Joe's passing. It was a chance to catch up, talk, and spend time together.

Between Pro's police duties and Elisha's work as a designer, they rarely had a chance during the week.

"Mom!" Pro yelled, and as usual headed toward her mother's bedroom to bring her the coffee in bed.

She pushed the door open to find her mother sitting up with the blanket pulled up to her neck. "Pro?" she exclaimed wide-eyed.

"Yeah," she said, and approached with the two cups, amused by her mother's behavior. "Why are you covering up? Did you have a hot flash and pull off your bedclothes or something?"

Pro froze as another shape moved in the bed just beyond where her mother lay.

Max's head sprung up, his hair tousled and standing up in odd places. He smiled, bleary-eyed. "Pumpkin? I hope that's coffee."

Pro sat at the small kitchen table and took another sip from her cup. She was still shaking. The uncontrolled rage wanted to burst out of her and strangle the bastard who had sired her.

Her mother finally came out in a nightgown and robe, then sat tiredly across from her.

"How… could… you…" Pro stammered.

"What do you mean?" Elisha said, and reached for the coffee. At first, Pro seemed unable to unclench the hand from her mother's cup. "You gonna give it to me, or do I have to pry it from your cold, dead fingers?"

Pro released the cup, and Elisha took a much needed sip.

"How could you? In the bed you and Dad shared —"

"And me and your father before that," Elisha said. "Look, it's been a long time since I've been with a man, and it is none of your business who I sleep with."

"But, that— that—"

"Careful, he is still your father."

"How could you dishonor Joe that way?"

Elisha looked at her daughter sympathetically. "Oh, honey, I would never dishonor your stepfather. He was a good man. But he's the one who died, not me."

"But with—" Pro gestured hopelessly.

Elisha grinned despite herself. "This was the one thing your father and I never had a problem with."

Max came into the room, tying the belt of a ratty robe as he entered. "Hey there!"

Pro jumped to her feet. "That's Dad's robe!"

Max looked at it. "I saw it behind the door, and I thought this was better than coming out in my underwear."

"It's fine," Elisha assured.

At the same moment Pro commanded, "Take it off!"

Max looked from one woman to another, and then at the robe he was wearing.

Elisha stood up herself, her eyes not leaving her daughter's. "This is my home, and I say he can wear it," she said in a menacing tone.

Max moved his head from one to the other as if he was watching a tennis match, but neither woman gave an inch.

"Anyone for waffles?" Max attempted. "Or did the waffle iron become Joe's as well?"

Elisha folded her arms, her eyes daring her daughter. "No, it's still in the kitchen."

"If you know where that is," snapped Pro.

"I know it will be a good place to hide," Max muttered, and hastily headed past the table and into the small kitchen.

"You'd best back off, honey," Elisha growled.

"He doesn't belong here," Pro returned icily.

"He does if I say so."

"I could cut up some fresh fruit," Max shouted from the kitchen. "Anyone care for that?"

Elisha took her index finger and slid Pro's cup toward her. "Now you sit down and drink your coffee, and be a polite young lady before I spank your ass."

"Huh," Pro huffed. "You never hit me as a child."

"Well, you never behaved like this. You are not too big for me to knock you down."

Pro slowly sat as she fought a desire to shake her mother violently.

Elisha stood up straight and lowered herself into her chair. "Fruit sounds nice, Max." She returned her eyes to her wayward child. "You want fruit?"

"I want you to stop being a doormat to that man."

This made Elisha smile. "Oh, honey, how little you understand me. And you really don't know your father at all."

"Maybe if he'd stuck around a little longer..." she seethed.

"Honey, you've got to let it go. Max did the best he could by us both. But all you see is what he didn't do."

"No, I was lucky enough to have a real man in my life—"

"And Joe adored you. But if you could only see how much you are like your father."

Pro leaped to her feet again. "I am nothing like him!"

Elisha smiled up at her daughter. "Personality-wise, you are exactly like him. All fire and hot. However, he's cooled down, mellowed. It wouldn't hurt you to calm down some too."

Pro slowly returned to her seat, just as Max came out with a plate of fruit. It was not only cut in bite-sized pieces, but each of the slices had been artistically cut into shapes. They resembled animals, flowers, and even a rather impressive elephant.

Max placed the fruit down and Pro stared at it. An unbidden tear suddenly came from her eye.

"Do you like it, Pro?" Max beamed. "I used to cut them like this for you when you were little."

Pro stared up in disbelief at her father, jumped up again, and ran to the bathroom as she stifled a sob, slamming the door as she went.

Max sighed. "She's a hard nut to crack." He sat at the table and picked at the fruit.

"Made herself hard because she thinks she has to be," Elisha said and offered Max her cardboard cup.

He smiled and gratefully took a sip. "I couldn't find the coffee maker."

"I have one of those single shot things with the little plastic cups," Elisha said as she rose and went around the table to head to the kitchen. "I'll make us both a cup."

In a quick move, Max took her hips and sat Elisha on his lap, and leaned her back to kiss her neck. "Don't leave me."

"Now stop, Max!" Elisha giggled. "If Pro sees this, it will just set her off again."

"I don't care! Last night was the first time in years I truly felt at home. That I was with someone who was just right."

She turned in his lap to face him. She moved in and kissed him, then pushed herself to arm's length.

"Max, last night was great fun…"

Max smirked. "I got that from all the moaning."

"But…" she said carefully, "it was not the beginning of something. Don't read more into it than what it was."

"Oh?"

"After all these years, I can say I have no anger at you and that I honestly like you."

"Last night seemed a lot more than just 'like,'" Max chuckled and kissed her neck again.

She pushed him back. "Max, last night was just a walk down memory lane." Elisha rose. "A lovely walk, but only that. However, the least I can do is give you a cup of coffee."

She headed into the kitchen. Max sighed and looked from the kitchen to the bathroom. "The two most important women in my life are insane," he muttered to himself.

Pro stepped out of the bathroom dry-eyed and stiff-backed.

"I have to go to work," Pro announced. "I am pulling Saturday shift."

"Oh, Pro, before you go," Max said, "I just wanted to discuss a few things about our case."

Pro stopped dead in her tracks and slowly turned to her father. "*Our* case?"

"Yes, I have a few ideas where we can go from here," Max said just as Elisha returned with a cup of coffee, prepared the way Max liked. He took a sip. "Oh, that is good, Elisha."

"Now you know why I switched," Elisha replied.

Pro put her hands on her hips. "Max, you have nothing to do with the case—"

"I know, but I think the way to go is to track down those illusion plans that were made of my trick. If we can locate the people interested in buying them—"

Pro held up a hand. "Max, we will go through Mister Floss's emails and follow up on everyone he had business dealings with. That is standard procedure."

"Pro, you don't get it. You are dealing with magicians! Whoever killed Floss knew when I was coming and set me up to take the fall!"

"Hard to believe—"

"Oh yeah? How did the police know to come to the shop?"

Pro leaned with one hand on her hip. "They got a call from the neighbor who said they heard noises in the shop."

"Which neighbor?"

"They didn't identify themselves, but we triangulated the signal of the cellphone and they were in the same building."

"Or in the hallway of the same building. I'm telling you, Pro, someone who understands the art of misdirection did this. You need my help."

"Max," Pro warned. "You need to stay out of this case, stay out of my office, and while you're at it, stay the hell out of my life!"

She looked at the plate of cut fruit and suddenly looked as if she would cry again. "You and your damn fancy fruit!"

She stormed out of the apartment as her parents watched her leave.

"Look what you did to our baby," Elisha said as she shook her head.

"What I did?" Max sputtered and indicated the plate. "I made fruit the way she liked it when she was a kid."

"After you left, I made Prophecy a plate of fruit. I never learned how you did that fancy cutting—"

"Oh, it's easy—"

Elisha held her hand up. "When I cut up the fruit, it wasn't like Daddy's. She cried for hours that night, because that's when she knew you were really gone."

Max looked at the closed door his daughter had just left through.

"I never knew…" he mumbled sadly.

She took his face and turned him to look at her. "And that's the problem. I think you'd better get going." She stood up and cleared the table.

"So soon?" Max said with a smile. "Now that we're alone, I thought we could find out if last night was just a fluke."

"I don't think so," Elisha said pleasantly as she took the plate of fruit back into the kitchen and put it in the fridge.

Max followed her, frustrated. "You know, this was always the problem in our marriage. I never knew where I stood with you. One minute you're hot and the next you're cold."

"I am not the one who left, Max."

Max looked at her, cinching the robe tighter. "Are you going to tell me last night wasn't beautiful? That it didn't feel…right? And I mean, you got dressed up for me. When I suggested I wanted to see the place, you invited me up. You want to tell me it meant nothing?"

She sighed and faced her ex-husband. "No, I won't deny that when I saw that look in your eyes — that wanting — it kindled a lot of old feelings. Yes, I wanted to be with you. I wanted you to make love to me."

"And it was great, wasn't it? I'm not just fooling myself, am I?"

She turned from him. "It was everything I remembered. The passion, the way you touched me —"

He moved close and wrapped his arms around her. "I'd like to do that again—"

"The problem is, today in the light, I'm remembering all the stuff that pushed us apart. It's all still there, Max." She slipped out of his grasp. "I'm taking a shower."

"I can wash your back," Max suggested.

"Actually, I would like you to be gone before I'm done," she insisted. "I know your number if I want to get in touch."

She headed into the bathroom. Max followed several steps behind to find the door shut in his face.

6. Zig-Zag

P ro was at her desk as she went over a printout. It was a list of the emails from Albert Floss' laptop. The NYPD cyber unit had gone through the machine and printed all the senders and recipients by heading, though it didn't contain the text of the email. She could ask for any specific one from the list now that they had access to his email accounts.

"Anything good?" Chu asked as he looked over her shoulder.

"A friend suggested looking for the person who was trying to buy that 'Prism' illusion."

"By any chance, was the friend your father?"

"Yeah, and at first I told him to get lost. However, once I thought about it, it seemed to make sense."

"Good thinking," Chu said and pointed at several entries that listed 'mmarvell' as the sender. "We tracked down the emails your father sent, and they are damning."

"How do you mean?"

"On one, he suggested he knew how to hide a body in ways no one could ever find it. This was among other threatening hints if Floss didn't sell him back his illusion plans."

"Doesn't help him look innocent," Pro said.

"Hard to believe the magic business is so cutthroat."

She turned in the chair to look at her partner. "Not at all. My father had to be incredibly secretive when he created an effect, selecting how many people were involved in building it. He often did prototypes himself, just to make sure no one else knew what he was working on. He really is an innovator."

"Sounds like you're proud of him."

"What? No!" Pro grimaced, embarrassed. "I'm just aware of what he's done. It's important to our case."

"So you saw him. Did you visit him?"

Pro's jaw set. "He was at my mother's."

"Really?" Chu said with a raised eyebrow.

She exhaled loudly. "He spent the night."

Chu was silent as this sunk in. Finally he asked, "You okay?"

"I'm annoyed that this is bothering me. For chrissakes, he brought out fruit, cut up the way he used to do it when I was a kid, and I started blubbering."

"Do you feel you're not in control?"

"Exactly! I had everything in my life all figured out, and then he shows up out of the blue. He used to do this to me after the divorce. I'd get used to things, get myself into a routine, then he'd come into town or fly me out to Vegas, and I would be an emotional mess for weeks."

"He is quite a presence. I noticed that yesterday," Chu said while shaking his head. "Do you need me to have us reassigned? We certainly have reasons to request it."

"No," Pro said and slapped her desk. "Dammit, I will not let him make me back off a case. And to be honest, Tom, I think my knowledge about magicians might help."

He nodded. "Okay. But if you feel you can't handle it, you let me know. And you are due some days off—"

"Vacations are for wimps," Pro said with a wave of her hand.

"Now that sounds like my partner," Chu chuckled and turned his attention to the paper in her hand. "So, anything popping for you?"

"Yes, I found repeated emails from one specific sender about 'the item.' Can we get the information from the cyber unit about who this person is?"

"I already did. It hit me as well. They should get back to us with a user soon."

"Well, from the return email address, it is in the United States, but it could be anywhere in the country."

"Or down the street. Did you finish the paperwork on the bodega shooting?"

"No, sorry, I wasn't quite done."

"Well, if you finish writing it up, I'll do the follow up with Cyber."

She gave a nod as Chu headed back to his nearby desk. Pro watched him go. He was a good partner and a great mentor, always looking ahead to what they needed.

The words her mother said suddenly ran through her head: "You could use someone in your life that would inspire a little fire."

Well, Chu wasn't that person. She admired and liked her partner, probably would take a bullet for him. But she didn't feel attracted to him on a physical level. In fact, there had been very little of that as she struggled to go from uniformed officer to detective. Her single-minded purpose shut out all the other aspects of her life.

At her workstation, she pulled up the report and typed on her keyboard, but her mind continued to wander.

She thought about her former lover, Julius Trent, back when she was at the police academy. He was a tall, African-American man with a shaved head and the body of a weight-lifter. During her training, they had a friendly competition that inspired both of them to work harder. It had consummated with nights of some very nice sex, satisfying if not exemplary.

Her last serious relationship had been with a street magician, Jamie Tobin, over a year ago. They met when she was a uniformed officer and looking into the murder of another performer. With Tobin's help, and Chu with his partner at the time, Detective Franks, she helped close that case. When the older Franks retired a month later, Chu asked her to be his new partner.

Over the next month she learned the ropes, and at night, Jamie brought forth a passion she didn't know she'd possessed. He hadn't been her type at all—thin, red-headed, and Irish—but the things he could do with those talented hands…

She shook her head to clear it. Why was she letting that memory come to her now? It was useless and only brought up feelings she didn't want to deal with. The relationship ended with his return to Ireland twelve months ago.

He'd been a magician. And magicians always leave.

Had it been an entire year since she'd last made love?

She sighed at her desk. Why was she letting herself dwell on this? Because her mother had not been with a man since Joe's death, which was two years. A part of her assumed her mother would just be celibate. Then she spent the night with Max, of all people.

All at once, it hit her. She realized a childish part of her wanted to see her parents get back together, to reunite them back into a family. She shook her head in disbelief that she allowed such silly feelings to take hold.

"You still on that report?" Chu said as he approached with a paper in hand.

"What?" Pro said, sitting up in her chair and wondering how much time had passed.

"I have a lead from Cyber. They traced the IP address of that email, and I have a name and a physical address. It's right here in Manhattan."

Pro stood up. "What's the name?"

Chu looked at the paper in his hand. "Malcolm Shaut."

"You're kidding!"

"No," Chu said and looked at the paper again to be sure. "Do you know him?"

"I know of him. He's the producer of A Night of Wonder down in the village. That's been running for like twenty-five years."

"What is that?"

"It's a show in an off-Broadway theater on Monday nights. It's a live stage presentation of magicians from all over the world, whoever is in town that week. Max would work there occasionally when he'd visit…"

"Pro, you have a glazed look in your eyes."

"Sorry. I was just thinking about how my father did that show. He would take me out to dinner and the show, even though it was a school night," Pro said, and her features grew hard. "I guess I didn't appreciate it back then."

"So, your memories aren't all bad," Chu suggested.

"I guess not. Where is this guy?"

"He's right nearby on 50th Street. Hell, we could walk to his place. It's right between Ninth and Tenth Avenue."

"And only a few blocks from our murder scene," Pro added.

"I noticed that as well."

They took their police vehicle and were soon walking up the long front steps of an impressive brownstone. There was a wrought-iron protective fence around the ground floor entrance. However, workmen had added fanciful designs to the metal bars resembling moons, stars, and wands. The windows facing the street also had the same protective ironwork up all three floors of the edifice.

"Does this guy own the entire building?" Pro asked.

Chu checked his paper. "It doesn't say. But there is only one buzzer."

Chu pressed a button on a metal plate with a speaker.

"Who is it?" a male voice snapped over the intercom.

"Detectives Chu and Thompson, NYPD. We need to speak with Mister Shaut."

"Show your badges to the camera. It's over the door."

The two detectives exchanged an annoyed glance. Together, they pulled out their billfolds and showed their shields to the small lens over the doorway that glimmered in the sunlight.

The door buzzed, and Pro opened the ten foot tall narrow door to walk through. A second door waited just three feet from the first, and Chu pushed through it.

A door opened at the end of the hall and Chu and Pro walked past an impressive stairway that led to the next floor. A thin, average height man with dirty-blond hair and a receding hairline stepped forward to meet the detectives, leaving the door ajar. As he drew near, Pro could see a small chin beard and mustache and guessed that he was about thirty but looked younger.

"Mister Shaut?" Chu asked.

"No, I'm Brent Williams, his assistant," the man said. "Let me take you to him."

He led Chu and Pro through the door, which faced a bathroom. However, with a slight shift to the left, they went into an open room which contained a large desk made of chrome and glass. There was a computer monitor on the glass top, and to the right and the left were short filing cabinets, also made from the shiny metal. Poised on a wheeled chair with a fancy leather seat was a fair-looking man with average features and graying black hair. He was clean shaven, wearing a pair of black pants with a light-blue shirt and a dark-blue sports coat. He carried the air of a performer as he looked away from the monitor and at his visitors.

"This is Mister Shaut," Brent announced, and headed off into a side room. Pro watched as he walked through a small waiting room with several chairs, a coffee table, and a television. He then passed through another doorway to a small office. His desk with computer and phone was clearly visible as he sat.

"Please show me your badges again," Shaut demanded.

"Shields, Mister Shaut," Pro corrected as she opened her leather billfold and held it out for the man. "Officers have badges, detectives have shields."

"Whatever." He shrugged. Facing him were two matching chrome and leather chairs, and he gestured to them. "Please sit and tell me what I can do for two of New York's finest."

Chu spoke first. "We wanted to speak to you about emails you were exchanging with one Albert Floss about an unnamed item."

"Christ," Shaut said, displeased. "Is Marvell sending the cops after me now?" He called out to his assistant, "You hear that, Brent, Marvell's sending the cops after us."

Brent walked back into the room carrying a mug emblazoned with the phrase "I'D RATHER MAKE RABBITS DISAPPEAR" and placed it in front of his employer, then added ruefully, "The man certainly has a problem, Mister Shaut."

"I'll say he does," Shaut said as Brent returned to the nearby room. "Look, detectives, he honestly doesn't have a leg to stand on—"

"You were in touch with Mister Marvell?" Pro interrupted.

"Yeah, and tell him if he makes any more threats, I'm going to have the Las Vegas Police visit him."

"Are you sure you are speaking about Max Marvell?" Chu queried.

"Yeah, isn't he the one who sent you? I mean, I know that he's buddies with the mayor, but that doesn't mean he can send detectives to harass me—"

Chu cleared his throat, and Pro let him take over.

"We aren't here for Marvell, Mister Shaut," Chu pointed out. "We are here because of your relationship with Albert Floss."

"What? Yeah, I know Al. He's been around forever. In fact, he was selling me information on a trick — an illusion."

"By any chance," Pro coaxed, "the Prism?"

Something clicked in Shaut's mind, and his eyes became narrow as he gazed at Pro. "Hey, I know you, those blue eyes. Now I know this is a scam. You're Max's kid, Prophecy." He rose from his chair and pointed at Pro, his face growing red. "I remember seeing you backstage when you were little! What are you two trying to pull—"

"Mister Shaut," Chu raised his voice to silence the man. "We are here because we are investigating the murder of Albert Floss."

Shaut stared at Chu, unbelieving. "Al's dead? Murdered?"

"Yes, sir, yesterday at 11:00 AM in his shop on—"

"I know where it is," Shaut disclosed as he flopped into his chair. "Who did it? Was it Max? Is that why you brought—" He pointed an accusing finger at Pro.

"Detective Thompson is my partner. We are the detectives assigned to the case."

"Thompson? Oh yeah, I heard your mom remarried," Shaut concluded and turned to Pro. "Glad you were smart enough to change your name."

Pro's mouth was a tight line as she pushed back her anger. "We are not here to discuss me, Mister

Shaut. We are here to ask you about your business arrangements with Albert Floss."

His hands went up defensively. "Whaddaya talkin' about? Everybody knew Al, and everybody did business with the old man."

Chu took over. "But you were emailing him about an item. May I ask what the item was?"

"Sure, it was like the broad said — it was Prism."

"Broad?" Pro fumed and rose from her seat. Chu put a restraining hand on her shoulder, and she slowly lowered into it, her blue eyes fixed angrily on Shaut.

"Sorry, uh… lady… uh… cop… detective, whatever you are," Shaut offered dismissively. "If Al ended up dead, you gotta look at Max Marvell. When he found out I was interested in Prism, he wrote me emails sayin' he was gonna sue my ass — and worse."

"Do you have copies of those emails?"

"Yeah. Hey, Brent!"

Brent stuck his head out dutifully. "Yes, sir?"

"Can you print those nutty emails that Marvell sent me for the detectives?"

"It would be my pleasure, Mister Shaut. It's about time someone took that man seriously."

"Yeah, I don't need the commentary, just do it!" Shaut barked and turned to his monitor. Pro and Chu could hear a laser printer hum to life in the next room.

"Mister Shaut, while you're doing that, can you print up the emails you sent to Albert Floss as well?" Chu coaxed.

"Ain't that something you need a warrant for?" Shaut asked, suspicious again.

Chu stood and leaned across the desk. "Not if you're willing to volunteer them. If not, and I have to get a warrant, I assure you, we will also search the entire house for anything suspicious."

Flustered, Shaut conceded. "Okay, okay. Brent!"

"I am on it, sir. I heard the detective."

"Good, good," Shaut responded, then added snidely, "the last thing I would want to do is inconvenience the NYPD."

Pro pulled out her notebook. "And where were you yesterday between ten and eleven in the morning, sir?"

"Me? Why are you asking me?"

"It helps us eliminate people," Chu claimed.

"I was here, right at this desk."

Pro made a note in her book. "You have anyone to verify that?"

"Brent, was I here yesterday between ten and noon?"

"Sorry, Mister Shaut, it was my half-day," Brent replied from the other room. He walked in. "However, you called me at about 10:30 to make an appointment in your online calendar and check the availability for that French magician in July."

Shaut grumbled. "Okay, well, Friday is when I send out my email flyer for the next Monday's performance. I have to write it up."

"I can verify that, detectives," Brent said helpfully. "When I came in at noon, I found a finished schedule. I just added the graphics and sent it out. It had not been ready when I left the previous night."

"Is there anyone else in this building?"

Shaut shook his head. "No, it's just Brent and me, and he doesn't live here."

"Really?" Pro demanded. "And how did a man who runs a magic show end up owning a brownstone in Manhattan?"

"Not that it's any of your business, detective," Brent grumbled defensively, "but Mister Shaut is a renowned software developer."

"Calm down, Brent, they have to ask. Yeah, I sold out my company to Google years ago and pursued my passion for magic. I have an entire workshop in the basement where I create my own effects."

Undaunted, Pro said, "When you're not stealing from Max Marvell?"

"Mister Shaut would never steal an effect," Brent spat haughtily. "He pays for them."

"Hey, I wanted to know how it works, that's all. I don't know if I would actually build the damn thing. I saw Max do it in Vegas. You're his kid; you've seen it."

Pro folded her arms. "Max and I haven't seen each other for years. So no, I haven't."

"Really? Well, let me tell you, girlie, this was the most amazing thing I ever saw. He is out there, on a stage, pretty much empty, except for a couple of glass whatchamacallits, like triangle shapes but flat on the ends."

Brent piped up, "It's a polyhedron with a triangular base."

"Whatever! So, he's out there with these two prism things on two rotating platforms, and there's a flash of rainbow light, real pretty, and he's gone, just freakin' gone. I watched the show from the orchestra. He's nowhere near a wall or a box or anything with a mirror. So, next night, I watch from the balcony, figuring he uses a trap door. Nothing. He just disappears. I want to know how it was done."

"And Albert Floss offered to sell you the secret?" Chu asked.

"Yeah, for fifty grand."

"Fifty grand?" Pro repeated. "You would spend that just to learn how a trick was done?"

Brent once again interrupted. "You don't understand, detective, it's not just a trick. It is the penultimate vanish of a human being on stage."

"I gotta agree with Brent," Shaut disclosed. "It's an impressive effect. Floss told me he could get copies of Marvell's design, and with his own information, he assured me I could do the trick. I could even do it on a smaller scale."

"By the way, detectives," Brent asked, "when you found Mister Floss, did you locate the plans?"

Pro folded her arms again. "It's an ongoing investigation. We are not at liberty to say."

Shaut grew very serious. "Well, if you don't find 'em, I gotta tell you, I would look seriously at Max Marvell."

"Mister Marvell is not your concern," Chu reported. "What is your concern is that you don't have an alibi for the time in question."

"Detective!" Brent bellowed.

Shaut held up his hands. "Hey, I wasn't the only interested buyer. One reason Al made the price so high is that he told me he had five guys interested."

"Do you know who they were?" Pro prodded.

"Not a clue. Magicians are a pretty tight-lipped group."

"May we have those emails, Mister Williams?" Chu asked of Shaut's assistant.

"Hm? Oh, yes," Brent mumbled and went into the side room to retrieve a sheaf of papers.

"We appreciate your time," Chu said. "We might be back to ask a few more questions once we've gone through these emails."

"Well, I think you realized the same thing I did," Shaut said, as he walked the two detectives to the door.

"What's that?" Pro asked.

"That Max Marvell is a dangerous guy."

7. Chain Escape

- -

A few minutes later, Chu was driving back to the 54th Street Precinct, as Pro looked over the dozen pages Shaut's assistant had given them.

"Anything good?" Chu asked, noting the silence of his partner.

"Nothing good for Max, I'm afraid. He makes frightening suggestions what he will do if Shaut doesn't comply."

"Such as?"

Pro leaned close to the paper. "I know where the bodies are buried. If you don't want to be one of them, you won't help Al cheat me." She slipped the page and went to a second one. "Once I take care of AF—I guess that's Albert Floss—you'll be next. And so on…"

"I emailed LVPD to see if there is any history of violence with your dad."

"Let's just call him Max," Pro said, her back stiffening. "He honestly is a stranger to me."

"A stranger who spent the night with your mom."

This made her even tenser. "Like I told you yesterday, my mom loses all sense when he is around. I'm still trying to deal with the fact they slept together. God! She might have slept with a murderer."

"Don't get too far ahead of yourself. So far, the only thing we can prove is that he was in the wrong place at the wrong time."

"And made threats," Pro grumbled while waving the papers.

"We assume he did, but we still need to tie the email address to Max. It would make sense to bring him back to interview again."

Pro shook her head. "This is why I loved my stepdad so much. He was a rock. When he and Mom married, my life became very stable."

"Some people would call that boring," Chu suggested.

"Not me. When Max came around, everything was crazy because he always had to run off to do gigs. Schedules would change on a dime. He would cancel promised events or parties. I had more than enough craziness when I was little. Joe was predictable. I liked that."

They pulled into their assigned parking space, and Chu turned off the car just as his phone rang.

"Chu!" he spoke into his phone, then listened. "We're on it."

Pro had stepped out of the car but stayed in place with the door open. She knew this meant. NYPD had assigned them another case and would be off again in a minute.

"We got another murder," Chu told her from the driver's seat.

"Of course we do," Pro said, and got back into the car.

"It's at another magic shop, so they sent it to us."

"Do you think it was our killer?" Pro said as Chu started the vehicle.

"According to the officers on site, a rope was used to strangle the vic," Chu stated as he maneuvered the car back into traffic. "And some of that special rope was lying on his chest — only this time it was blue."

It was a quick drive to 52nd Street near Broadway, a few hundred feet from a Gallagher's Steak House. The pair of detectives soon walked up to the second floor of an office building

The hallway had several similar doors, each with a different sign that listed the business. One sign read "Talent Agent"; another had a paper printed on a laser printer and claimed to be an "App Developer." At the end of the hall was a laminated notice that bore a magic wand and the words, "Tanner's Magic."

They walked into a much cleaner and brighter space than Albert Floss's shop had been. Like Floss, there was shelving all along the walls of the room, but it wore a fresh coat of white and was clear of any dust.

The equipment that lined the walls looked new and well-maintained, and the glass cases were undamaged, the glass polished. Cards, coins, and round balls made of sponge filled the cases. There were also display boxes that contained tricks, the artwork was modern, and the copy printed on the boxes suggested, "Anyone can do it!"

There was a uniformed officer carrying a roll of yellow tape that was printed with the words "CRIME SCENE" in bold, black letters. She was a good-looking woman with auburn hair pulled back in a ponytail and her blue eyes watched everything. She had an impressive figure, and when Chu looked at her, she lowered her eyes and smiled a secret smile.

"Detectives," she said. "You got here fast."

"Officer Barker, good to see you." Chu smiled. "What have we got?"

"Without forensics, it's just a guess." She led them through a break between two display cases, and when she turned, they saw the body of a man on the floor between a display case and the wall shelves. The man had a full head of hair and was stout and not as tall as Floss had been. He wore a simple white shirt and black pants and lay on the floor with his mouth hanging open, exposing several gold teeth.

There was a red line around his neck where the flesh was raw.

"It appears the perp strangled the vic, possibly garroted him with a blue rope that we found on his chest. However, there was a wit on the scene who called it in. He keeps saying that it isn't really rope. He also identified the vic as Louie Tanner."

Pro recognized the term "wit" as police shorthand for "witness," and all at once she had a tightness in the pit of her stomach. "Someone called it in?"

"Yes, detective," Barker said, turning to Pro. "Claims he found the DB and touched nothing. The strange thing is that he called the precinct directly instead of 9-1-1." She gestured to a doorway behind the counter. "He's back there with my partner, if you want to talk to him."

"Do you think it's—" Chu muttered.

"It better not be," Pro fumed as they walked past the counter and into a storage room.

They moved into the clean back room where two men sat. One was Barker's partner, Officer Bailey, who was tall and well-proportioned. The top of his head was bald, and he had brown hair on the sides and around his ears.

Sitting next to him was Max Martin, aka Max Marvell.

He stood as the two detectives entered. "Pumpkin!" he bellowed, and immediately corrected himself. "I mean Detectives Chu and Mar — uh — Thompson."

The magician was now wearing dark pants, either navy blue or black, a brown jacket, and a turtleneck.

Chu's face grew quite stern. "Officer Bailey, please join your partner in securing the scene."

The officer saw the looks in the detectives' eyes and didn't need to be told twice. He bolted from the back room.

"What the hell?" Pro yelled, and with a glance back at the retreating Bailey immediately lowered her voice. "What are you doing here?"

"It was like I was trying to tell you this morning —"

"I'd rather not go into what happened this morning," Pro interrupted.

"But that's just it," Max continued, undaunted. "This was what I thought would be the next step in the chain. Lou Tanner was trying to purchase Prism from Al Floss—"

Chu held up his hand to stop Max from talking. "Mister Martin, do you realized that this is the second murder scene where we discover you alone with a dead body?"

Max considered this. "Yes."

Chu's mouth was a firm line. "Do you know what that means?"

"Sure," Max replied airily. "It means I'm on to something!"

"No," Chu stated emphatically. "It means you are under arrest. Please turn around."

Max exhaled heavily. "You can't believe I had anything to do with—"

Pro stepped up to her father, and in a quick movement, turned him and bent him over a nearby table that had a chipped coffee cup atop it. She took out a pair of plastic restraints and fastened his arms behind him. Her fury was obvious. "When my partner tells you to do something, I'd advise you to do it!"

"Ow! Pro you're hurting me!" Max objected.

"Not as much as I want to, old man," Pro seethed as she finished restraining him. "There! And these are plastic double-cuff restraints — they don't use a key. Let's see you pick those, Max."

Chu stepped from the room, but they could hear him talking to the uniformed officers. "Did you call this into forensics?"

"Yes, detective," the woman replied. "And the medical examiner."

"Good work," Chu encouraged. "Detective Thompson and I are taking this suspect into custody."

"Roger that," Bailey replied.

Pro pulled her father upright and pushed him toward the doorway.

"You're making a mistake. I can help," Max whined.

"You have the right to remain silent, Max," Pro said, pushing him along. "So shut the hell up."

"Go over it again, Mister Martin," Chu said an hour later as he rubbed his forehead and took another sip of bad coffee from a cardboard cup.

"I told you the story, twice," Max said, his hands still behind his back as he sat in the same interrogation room as yesterday. "And I even did it without my lawyer present. That has to show good faith."

"Let's be clear, Mister Martin, you are spending tonight in a cell. If you behave, I'll take those restraints off."

"Oh, these?" Max brought his hands in front of his body and deposited the closed restraints on the table. "I only stayed in them so that Pro — um — Detective Thompson wouldn't get upset. Does she always act like this, or is it just me?"

"It's definitely you," Chu affirmed, and found he couldn't help himself. He picked up the interlocking plastic loops to examine them. "We have to cut these to release a prisoner. We have a special tool…"

Turning them over in his hands, Chu couldn't find any way that Max had cut or damaged the restraints.

He was simply no longer in them.

"Yes, that's what makes getting out of them more difficult, but also more amazing, don't you think?" Max suggested.

Chu slammed the restraints onto the table. "This isn't a joke, Mister Martin. Two people are dead, and we have copies of threatening emails sent by you to two different people. What are the odds that when our cyber unit goes through Mister Tanner's emails, they will find messages you sent to him?"

"The odds are good. But as I tried to explain it to Pro, you have to be aware of the misdirection. Someone is doing everything they can to point suspicion at me."

"That sounds like paranoia, Mister Martin," Chu replied.

"But as I told you, I called Louie and set up the appointment with him after I left my apartment — I mean Mrs. Thompson's apartment this morning. It was just going to be a friendly chat. Lou and I are old friends. I thought together we could figure out the identity of the man who stole my trick."

"I thought Albert Floss stole your trick," Chu asserted.

Max shook his head. "He was just the middleman. Al was good, but he doesn't have the knowledge to recreate an illusion on the level of Prism." Max leaned back in this chair. "But Lou, he'd have the inside knowledge of who in New York could do it. Don't you see? That's why they killed him. He probably figured out who recreated the techniques of my effect."

"This is all well and good, but so far, you're the only constant in this case. Everything points to you!"

Max went on. "I'm telling you, find the man who drew those plans, and you will have your killer."

"Unfortunately, that appears to be you, Mister Martin. End interview!"

Chu stood up from the chair, took his folder with him, and stepped to the door as Pro buzzed it open.

He slammed the door behind him and pointed at a nearby officer. The man was very tall, at least six-foot-eight. He had a square chin and a taut, lean body that gave the appearance of a normal man stretched out to the extended height. "Jacobs?"

"Yes, sir, detective."

Chu pointed his thumb at the door he'd just exited. "Get this man into holding and be alert. He's tricky."

"Yes, sir," the officer said and walked to the door, which Pro buzzed open.

Using his long arms, Jacobs held the door open and guided Max out, taking him in the direction of the precinct's holding cells.

"Tom," Pro said as her annoyed partner drew near. "What if he's... I dunno... on to something?"

"What he's on to is a rap for two counts of Murder One," Chu griped. "I hope he enjoyed his one day outside, because I think I will keep him in a cell from now on."

"Can we hold him?"

"Up to seventy-two hours on suspicion. I intend to use every hour of that."

"Okay," Pro said and turned away, suddenly feeling guilty.

"Look, Pro, it's for his own good," Chu explained, sensing his partner's conflict. "If he's here in a cell and other magicians get killed with the same MO, it will exonerate him."

"I see that," Pro divulged to her partner. "I just don't know what to do with him here. He makes me so angry, and then I feel guilty that I get mad. A part of me wants to strangle him and another part just wants to sit down with him over coffee."

"So you have mixed feelings."

"Very mixed. And I don't like it. I'm usually the person in control."

Chu sat at the corner of Pro's desk. "I know, and you've got the smarts that keep your temper in check. But this has been a struggle for you."

She shook her head. "I all but lost it this morning when I went to Mom's apartment and there he was. I felt like all the years where Joe worked so hard to give us a life and a strong family had been erased by an intruder."

"Family can be difficult," Chu pondered. "I mean, my parents are traditional Korean. Every day after school, I had violin lessons and Tae Kwon Do. When I went into law enforcement as a cop instead of becoming a lawyer, you would have thought I had committed a high crime. To this day, my folks are always comparing me to their friends' more successful children, who are doctors and lawyers."

"At least your parents stayed together."

"Yeah, and there were other advantages. I acted as my parents' translator from the time I could talk, which came in very handy at parent-teacher meetings. But our parents are who they are, just like we have to be who we are." He shrugged. "I'm a cop."

"Mom wasn't happy when I went to the academy, but Joe was so proud I would've sworn he was gonna bust."

"And I'm sure Max is proud of you, too."

Pro sighed. "I guess so. Man, so many memories have been coming back since he arrived. He was right. I told him I didn't want to see him anymore when I was a teenager. I guess that hurt him."

"You were angry because he left you and your mom."

"And I never understood why Mom didn't get angry about it."

"Maybe she did and didn't want to let you see it."

Pro paused and looked at the floor in thought. "I think maybe it's time I talked to her about it."

"Might be the right time," Chu said, and glanced over as Jacobs walked into the room. "Where did he end up, Jacobs?"

Jacobs moved closer and peered down at Chu and Pro. "I came by to tell you he's in holding cell three, but it was strange, detective."

"Strange in what way?" Chu responded.

"You know how a prisoner turns over all his belongings at the processing desk? Well, all of his pockets were empty: no wallet, no money, only a pair of glasses—said he needs them to read."

Pro stood. "Nothing in his pockets? How about a deck of cards?"

Jacob frowned. "Nothing."

Pro looked at the tall officer and her eyes moved to his chest, which showed both of the pockets of his uniform in one unbroken space of very dark blue.

"Crap, crap, crap," Pro muttered.

Chu stared at his partner. "What is it?"

"C'mon," Pro pressed urgently and moved. "We have to check on him right now."

"What?" Chu said, confused but following Pro. "He's in holding. Where could he go?"

"It's Max, dammit. Misdirection," Pro said as they walked through the hallways quickly.

"What'd you mean?" Chu wondered. "What does misdirection have to do with him being in holding?"

"His pants," Pro said as she picked up the pace.

"What about them?"

Pro stopped in the hall near the processing desk. "They had a stripe down them. I didn't think about it until I looked at Jacobs' uniform."

Chu frowned. "What was wrong with his uniform? He looked fine to me."

Pro lowered her voice. "His badge backer was missing."

"What?"

"Sh! His badge backer, the thing that holds his badge, name tag, and citation ribbons."

"I know what it is. I was in uniform once."

They turned and headed to lockup, where a very heavy steel door waited. An NYPD officer watched the door and had to buzz them in.

As they stepped into holding, which was in a 'T' shape, there was a center corridor with cells on both sides. This went ten feet and split into two passageways, one to the right and one to the left, and more cells. Pro leaned over to peek at the lock on the first barred door.

"Will you tell me what is going on?" Chu said, annoyed.

"I'm afraid you'll see for yourself in less than a minute," Pro said, her voice tense. She walked up to holding cell number three, which was to the right at the corner where the hallway split.

It was empty.

Chu looked into the unoccupied cell. "So, Jacobs got the wrong number."

"I'll wait here. Check at the processing desk."

Chu shook his head and walked to the locked door, which was opened by the officer on the other side. He walked to the processing desk. Behind the counter were monitors with a camera trained on the ten different-sized cells in the holding area.

"Where did Max Martin end up?" Chu asked the man behind the desk.

The officer had gray hair and a heavy mustache and seemed to think he was the Latin-lover type with his slicked back hair. "Him?" the man said with a slight accent. "He ended up in a nice solo — holding cell three."

"He's not there," Chu said.

"Yeah, right," the man chuckled. "Don't tell me. He disappeared. Come on, detective, I got work to do."

"I'm serious," Chu said. "The cell is empty."

The man's demeanor changed, and he grew serious. He rose from the desk and grabbed a set of keys. "Hey, Tony, I gotta check somethin'."

The man stood and came through a nearby door, as Tony took his place at the desk. He joined Chu, and the two went down the hall to the locked door and soon stood before the empty cell with Pro.

The processing desk officer, who wore sergeant stripes and a name tag that read "PALOS," used his keys to open the door and the three cops stepped into the empty cell.

"Geez!" Palos said. "I thought you guys were pullin' my leg."

Pro stepped past the befuddled sergeant and went right to the bed that was bolted to the wall. It appeared rumpled, and she quickly pulled it up. Under the mattress, she located the brown jacket and the turtleneck Max had been wearing.

"That guy really was a magician," Sergeant Palos proclaimed. "He just friggin' disappeared!"

8. Book Test

Within fifteen minutes, they formed a hastily assembled group that included Pro, Chu, Officer Jacobs, as well as Sergeant Palos. Since there had been such a breach of security, Lieutenant Dunton had also been called in.

Pro had promised an explanation. She sat in front of the monitors as a man sitting at the computer keyboard replayed several videos from earlier.

"It was the pants that clued me. I thought nothing of it when we picked him up at the crime scene, but once we got him into interrogation, I knew there was something wrong with them. Play the tape of the interrogation," she said to the man at the keyboard.

It showed Max talking to Chu.

"There, freeze it," Pro said. "Look at his pants. Can you blow that up?"

The image grew larger.

"Look at the color. It is a dead-on match for NYPD Blue, the standard issue uniform used all over the city. I don't know where he got it, maybe went to a uniform store or something. And look at the stripe down the side."

"I can barely see it," the Lieutenant grumbled from the back of the room.

"It isn't very obvious, even when a cop is in full uniform," Pro said. "Now play the video of holding cell three."

The image was of the front of the cell, and Jacobs brought Max in; Plastic cuffs restrained Max's hands in front of his body.

"Hold it," Chu said.

The video stopped moving again.

"When did those get put on him?" Chu said.

"When I took him out of interrogation, he was already in them," Jacobs explained. "I assumed you did it."

Pro looked at Chu. "Those must have been the ones from which he'd already escaped. You and I were talking, so neither of us saw him slip them back on. Keep going."

On the video, Max turned out as the door was closed and offered his hands. Jacobs pulled a tool from his belt and bent to get close to Max's hands, restrained by the bars.

"Hold it," Pro said. "Zoom in."

The photo grew larger, and Max's hands were touching Jacobs' badge backer.

"That's when he lifted the badge and credentials," Pro explained. "While you were taking the restraints off, he was swiping your badge. Continue!"

The video moved forward again, and Max expertly lowered his hands with the badge and blocked it with his body as Jacobs stood and walked out with the cut restraints. Max walked out of camera view toward where the bed and the open toilet sat.

"Do we have cameras in that part of the cell?" the lieutenant asked.

"No, sir," grumbled the officer at the computer. "That corner cell has limited visuals."

"I believe the suspect knew that from the previous day when he had been put in the same cell," Pro suggested.

"Great," the lieutenant said with crossed arms. "So, how did he get out?"

As the Lieutenant spoke, Max crossed back to the cell door and hung his hands through the bars and hung his head, as if depressed by his state of affairs.

"Freeze it," Pro demanded. "Now blow up the area around his hands."

The picture grew larger, and the hands filled the screen. When looking at the regular image, all you noticed was a man looking sad. But now that the hands were the focus, you could see a slender rod going into the door lock.

"What is that? What is he doing?" Chu said.

"He's picking the lock," Pro explained, "and he tried to look depressed to draw the attention of anyone watching away from his hands."

"But where did he get picks?" Sergeant Palos complained.

Pro sighed. "I'm guessing, but I would suggest he brought tools in one or both of the heels of his shoes."

"Geez!" Palos barked. "How were we supposed to know that?"

"Keep going on the video," Pro said. "I think the answer is that we weren't expecting this. But Max... Mister Martin... was."

On the video, Max stepped away from the door and back into the hidden part of the room.

"Focus on the door," Pro told the man at the keyboard. "I believe it was open at this point."

The keyboard operator moved the zoom in, and when the image drew closer, you could see that the door was slightly ajar.

"I'll be damned," the lieutenant muttered.

"Still, that doesn't explain how he got out of there," Palos noted.

"We're coming to that," Pro said. "Zoom back."

The camera view moved to the standard view of the cell. A totally different man moved into the frame inside the cell. He seemed taller and walked with confidence. The hair was different, black and short, not the slightly longer cut Max wore. But he was in an NYPD uniform, complete with badge, name tag, and badge backer on the left front of the shirt and NYPD patches on both arms.

The man walked to the door, opened it, and stepped into the hall, where you could now see a pair of glasses on his face. Between the glasses and the hair, it didn't look like Max Martin, aka Max Marvell, at all.

"Move the view to the outer door, same time frame," Pro said.

The monitor switched views, and the man stepped to the door. An officer on the other side glanced over and opened it, and the disguised Max stepped through the door and out of camera range.

"So the bastard disguised himself as an NYPD officer?" Lieutenant Dunton snapped. "So was that how he got out? He just traipsed out of here?"

Pro's jaw tightened. "I think so, LT. My supposition is that he wore a shirt with NYPD patches on the arms under his turtleneck. Once he pinched Officer Jacobs' badge backer, it was all he needed to look like a cop. You noticed he wore a wig. I can only assume he hid it in his jacket's lining or in the small of his back. It wouldn't set off a metal detector."

The lieutenant rose first. "Okay, first thing. The information that he escaped and how he did it does not leave this room!"

There was a murmur of agreement from the other officers.

"Christ!" Dunton went on. "If this gets out to the press, we are going to be a laughingstock and Internal Affairs will be all over our ass!"

"Yes, sir," Sergeant Palos said from his seat. "Should we issue an APB?"

"That goes without saying," Dunton snarled. "The all-points bulletin should include that he might be disguised as a police officer."

"Sir, that won't be necessary," Pro said. "I think he will dump the disguise as soon as possible."

"Include that anyway," Dunton demanded. "Now, Pro, I heard a rumor that this guy is your father. Is that correct, detective?"

"My biological father, sir, yes," Pro responded.

"Well, if you get word to him, by whatever means, you tell him to surrender himself... and quickly, or he is going to be in a cell for a very long time. We have him for resisting arrest, impersonating a police officer, assaulting a police officer—"

"He didn't assault me, LT," Jacobs said defensively.

"Shut up, Jacobs," Dunton ordered. "He stole your badge! You better pray I don't have you walking a beat for the next ten years."

"Yes, sir," Jacobs muttered sullenly.

The lieutenant turned back to Pro and Chu. "And I think personal feelings are impeding you two from doing your job."

"Sir, it's my fault," Pro said. "I wasn't as diligent as I should have been—"

"Put a sock in it, detective," Dunton roared. "I'll give you two forty-eight hours to solve these murders and capture that second-rate magician—"

"LT, Max Marvell is not a second-rate magician, sir," Pro objected. "That's why he fooled an entire precinct of officers."

Dunton's face became an unhealthy shade of red. "Just find him!" he hissed through clenched teeth, then stormed out of the room.

The meeting broke up, and Pro and Chu headed back to the bullpen.

"Tom, I am so sorry…"

"Why? You didn't know he was going to do this." He stopped and looked at her. "I mean, you didn't, did you?"

"No," Pro vowed, "and I can't figure out where he would have gotten NYPD arm patches. You can't just go into a store and ask for them."

"I have no idea. But we'd better catch Max—and fast. He's now a fugitive, and if someone is a little too trigger-happy, it could end badly."

Pro stopped walking, her face frozen in realization.

"What?" Chu asked, surprised by the look on her face.

"Mom!"

"What?"

"I have to call my mother," Pro said and moved away from her partner.

"Ask if she's seen Max, will you?"

Pro walked to a quieter corner of the precinct and pulled out her cell phone and hit the memorized number. Elisha picked up on the first ring.

"Mom, it's Pro."

"Yes, dear. Are you coming for dinner?"

"What? No, no," Pro said, remembering that Saturday night was typically dinner with her mom. "Have you heard from Max?"

"No, honey, we had a fight this morning after you left, so I told him I'd call him."

"A fight, why? I thought you two were all lovey-dovey?"

"Again, I feel no need to explain my relationship with your father."

"He snuck out of a holding cell and is now considered a fugitive."

"Oh, my!"

"If you hear from him, you tell him to turn himself in."

"How did he escape?"

"That's what I am calling about. When I made detective, I gave you a couple of old uniforms to hold on to, as I didn't have space."

"I don't have any idea how you live in that tiny apartment—"

"Mom, I don't want to argue. I want you to go see how many of my uniform shirts you have, and tell me where they are."

"Why do you need to know that?"

"There should be four. Can you please check?"

"Oh, all right. But I don't see what this has to do with anything," Elisha said as she banged doors.

Pro waited patiently as she heard footfalls and noises over the phone.

"I have them in my bedroom in Joe's old closet. There are three shirts here."

"I see. By any chance, was Max alone in your bedroom after I left?"

"I took a shower and told him to be gone when I was done. He was."

Pro nodded. Now she knew where Max had gotten the arm patches for his fake uniform. He'd stolen one of her shirts. She felt her temper rise. Not only had Max thought she would arrest him, he'd counted on it. It explained why he didn't ask for his lawyer on the second arrest. He'd already planned his escape.

But why? Because he could. It was just like her father to pull a childish prank that he thought was funny, but that screwed with her life.

It was like the time during one of his visits to New York. It was Pro's ninth birthday, and he had invited the birthday girl and some of her friends to his hotel to do a magic show, accompanied by several of the parents. Pro was so excited to present her famous father to her friends.

The show had been great fun, with classic effects, like the Chinese rings and the appearance of a live bunny. It captivated both the adults and the children as they applauded over and over.

But at the end, Max had moved to the front of the room and held up a large, elaborate cloth.

"And now," he intoned, "for my final effect!"

He moved to a doorway between the two rooms of the suite he had rented and held up the cloth, which filled the entire doorframe.

"Now count out loud to three!" Max said from behind the cloth.

The excited children yelled out, "ONE, TWO, THREE!"

There was a puff of smoke and the cloth fell to the ground, empty. At first, the children were stunned. Then one parent carefully rose and went through the doorway.

"He's not here!" she called from the other room.

Just then there was a knock at the door, and the children all looked surprised. Pro carefully went to the door and opened it.

Someone in a chef's outfit pushed in a cart. He wore a large floppy hat that hid his face. On the cart was an elaborate multi-tiered birthday cake, with sparklers burning atop it.

The children squealed, Pro among them.

The lights in the room suddenly went out, so the only light was from the sparklers.

"This looks delicious," the chef's voice croaked. "But not as delicious as YOU!"

With that, the chef pushed his hat back to reveal a scary clown face. His features twisted in wicked delight, and the face seemed to project an evil malice.

The sparklers all went out, plunging the room into darkness, as the children and several of the adults screamed in terror. One little girl wet herself.

And just as suddenly, the lights came up. The chef was still there, but he wore Max's face. The scary clown mask was gone, along with the large floppy hat. Max took a bow as the children sniffled and cried.

"How dare you!" one angry parent yelled as Max took off the chef's costume.

Her friends were still hysterical and all of them left, and no one had the cake except Max and Pro.

Max looked at his daughter and shrugged. "Sorry, pumpkin, I thought it was a wonderful trick."

At school the next week, her friends avoided her and wouldn't speak about the party. The one girl who had the "accident" never spoke to her again, and Elisha had to deal with angry calls from parents for days.

And, of course, Max flew back to Vegas and didn't have to deal with the upset and turmoil he'd left in his wake.

Pro shook herself to get past the memory and resentment to focus on her mother.

"Mom, do me a favor," Pro sighed. "Try to call Max. Tell him to surrender. They are putting out an APB on him."

"I will, dear," Elisha told her daughter. "I'm sorry this has been so upsetting for you."

"It will be more upsetting for all of us if Max gets himself shot."

9. Between Two Minds

P ro sat at her desk and went through the list of Albert Floss's emails a second time. Although the actual email wasn't there, it noted the sender, recipient, and the subject line. She used different colored highlighters to track repeated email conversations.

She looked over at her partner, who sat at his nearby desk going over a copy of the same list.

"So," Pro said, which made Chu raise his head, "Floss wasn't the person who made the plans. Is that our current theory?"

"That was the one Max put forth before his vanishing act," Chu responded sardonically. "I don't know if that is true or whether he was just saying it as a distraction."

"We have no reason to doubt he was sincere, do we?"

"Pro, your father has been pulling our chain since we discovered him in Floss's shop. Did your mother know where he is?"

"No, she said she hadn't heard from him. I checked the Waldorf-Astoria—"

"Right, that's where he said he was staying. Not bad digs."

"Yeah, he likes to project an image. Anyway, I spoke to a manager and they say he checked out."

"How did you get them to tell you that? The Waldorf never gives out information about their clients."

"Simple. I told the manager I was his daughter."

Chu shrugged. "Well, you didn't lie."

"They claim he left no forwarding address."

"The APB won't help us if he's holed up in a hotel somewhere."

"If he paid cash, no."

"By the way, I finally heard from Las Vegas PD."

"And?"

"They arrested Max for assault about two years ago in Vegas. He made threats and busted up some stuff at a magic store, claimed the owner stole one of his tricks."

Pro frowned. "Really?"

"The case was eventually pleaded out, and Max did a show for the Policemen's Benevolent Association as part of his community service."

"I guess that's nice."

"It's not good, Pro. It shows a history of violence when he thinks someone is stealing one of his tricks."

She shook her head. "I never knew that about him."

Chu leaned back in his chair. "I think what we have to do is try to expect his next move."

"That's why I've been correlating this list," Pro sighed. "If we can find out who designed the plans, then we might have the killer."

"If it isn't Max."

She shook her head. "I would have told you it was impossible this morning. But after the caper he planned and executed to get out of the cell, now I'm not sure." Pro's eyes returned to the sheet. "Do you know who this is? The email address is btg@magic.us. It seems like Floss was sending a lot back and forth to him."

"I got it on my list, but when I pull up the emails that cyber sent me from Floss's computer, it seems to be gibberish."

"What do you mean?"

"It's the same words over and over with some hyphens in it, not even modern words. Things like 'pray-answer' and stuff."

Pro spun in her chair to face her partner. "Print me up one of them. Let me look."

Chu hit the print button on his computer and a page spat out of the nearby laser printer. Chu handed it over to Pro, who looked at the page:

From: btg@magic.us

To: al@flossmagic.com

Subject: RE: Be Quick Twice Tell-Be Quick Tell-Be Quick Twice Pray-Be Quick Quickly, Say-Be Quick Be Quick Pray-Be Quick Twice
Message:

Be Quick Twice-Quickly-Tell, Please-Tell-Tell Look-Be Quick Look, Pray-Be Quick Look Be Quick Be Quick Say-Tell, Pray-Speak-Be Quick Quickly-Tell-Tell-Now.

Look, Be Quick Be Quick Say-Look-Be Quick Answer-Be Quick Answer, Say-Be Quick Twice Pray-Be Quick Twice, Be Quick Be Quick Tell-Be Quick Tell-Be Quick Twice Pray, Look-Be Quick Now

Pro stared at the odd message. "Wow, I see what you mean."

Chu nodded. "Our guys sent it to the State Cyber Crime Unit to see if it was some kind of embedded code, but they have found nothing so far. They even sent it to Cryptography to see if they could break it."

Pro stared at it. "Are they able to track down the real name of the sender?"

"No. The site that he's using as part of the address doesn't exist, yet someone owns the domain name. Some of the cyber guys suggested it is a dark website," Chu said and slapped the paper in Pro's hands. "And all we got is this gobbledygook."

Pro looked at the paper again and squinted. "Yet there's something familiar about this."

"Really? Any theories?"

"Seems like something my father told me about when I was little, but I can't quite remember."

Chu glanced at his watch. "Well, it's Saturday night, and since I have until Tuesday when you and I will be back in uniform pounding a beat—"

"The LT's angry, Tom, he's not crazy. We have a very good case closure rate."

"Even so, I want a night off from magicians, murder, and your crazy father."

"Me, too," Pro sighed and raised her eyebrows. "So, you and Barker, huh?"

Chu froze in place and slowly turned, then hurried over to Pro's desk. He leaned down. "How did you know I'm going out with Barker?" he whispered hoarsely.

"Oh, come on," Pro murmured back. "I saw how you looked at her, and more important, the way she looked at you. And to be honest, I didn't know, but now I do."

"You gotta keep it under wraps! You know how the LT hates it when cops date each other—"

"Hush, partner. I got you covered. Also, I like her. She's got good cop instincts."

"Thanks, Pro."

"I just don't understand what a good-looking lady like her sees in you," Pro teased.

"To be honest, neither do I, but I'm not complaining," Chu replied. "The only hard part is if it gets serious—I have no idea how to introduce her to my parents."

Pro frowned. "She's nice. What's the problem?"

Chu threw up his hands. "She's not Korean."

This made Pro laugh, the first time she had since this whole mess started. "Good night, Tom."

"Goodnight, Pro," Chu said with a vague wave as he went.

Pro turned back to the paper. She looked around the bullpen, but she was the only person left. There would be detectives on the weekend night shift, but they were probably at a crime scene.

Since she was alone, an idea struck her. She rose from her chair; the paper clutched tightly in her hand, and cleared her throat.

"Ahem!" she said, making her voice as deep and manly as possible. "Be Quick Twice-Quickly-Tell. Four score and Please-Tell-Tell Look-Be Quick Look —"

She stopped as a memory flooded into her mind. Sitting on the sofa in the apartment — her mother's apartment — no; she was little, and it was still her mother and father together. So she had to be about five.

She was sitting on the sofa with a doll in her hand. It was Barbie, and she also had a dark-skinned doll named Christie. Although the skin tone was African-American, the facial features were almost an replica of Barbie's.

"Hey, pumpkin," her father said as he came into the room.

"Hi, Daddy," Pro said. "I liked the show you took me to last night. It was fun."

"Yeah," her father said, all smiles. "It's fun to perform at Evening of Wonder. Wish it paid better."

"I liked the two people who went on before you," Pro said, and she brought her voice low as if imparting a secret. "They can read minds."

This caused him to burst into a loud laugh, which frustrated young Prophecy.

"They can't read minds, pumpkin," Max chuckled. "It's all a trick."

Pro scrunched up her face and crossed her arms. "But I saw them do it, Daddy."

"It's a two-person mentalist act," Max said dismissively. "They just coded each other the answers."

"They did what?"

Max smiled and relaxed. "I'm sorry, pumpkin, I didn't explain it well." He bent down, opened his arms, and picked Pro up to settle her on his hip. "C'mon, I'll tell you how it is done."

"Am I gonna know the sucrets, Daddy?"

"The secrets, yes. Because I want you to grow up and know that when people say they can read minds, it's all pretend."

"Like a fairy story, Daddy?"

"Yes," Max said, and carrying the little girl, he walked over to a bookcase and extracted a thick hardcover book with his free hand. He then sat on the couch and put Prophecy on his lap.

"What's the book, Daddy? Are there pictures?"

"This is the Kellock book about Harry Houdini," Max explained and opened to a page of the yellowing book to show a black-and-white picture of the famed conjuror.

"Does he do what you do, Daddy?" Pro asked, and snuggled close to her father, the smell of his aftershave in her nose. It made her feel safe, her tall father, who was magical.

"He did, but he died a long time ago. Here is what I want to show you." He flipped open to a page that listed numbers and words.

"What's that?" Pro pointed at the page.

"This was the code Harry used when he did a mentalist show with his wife, Bess. They had words that meant numbers, and they used the words to know what the other person wanted them to know. They call that a code." Max cleared his throat. "Harry would say things like: 'Be Quick, Bess.'"

His voice became deep when he became Harry, which made his daughter giggle. He then pointed at the open book. "See, and here in the book 'Be Quick' means the number 10."

"Uh-huh," Prophecy said. "So the man said things only the lady understood!"

"That's right, sweetie. You're so smart." He picked up the giggling girl and deposited her on the sofa. He then handed her Barbie and Christy, kissed her head, and headed for the room he used as an office.

Prophecy watched him walk away, smiling. She did not know that in six months he would be gone and her blissful life would be over. It would be years of shuttling to visit her dad, and her mother trying to be all things, but never able to achieve it. Until Joe walked into their lives and gave both women the love and stability they needed.

Pro looked around the empty bullpen and wiped the unexpected tear from her eye. "Damn that bastard," she muttered. "Here's another time for him to make me cry. Just like when I was a kid."

But the memory was clear in her mind. She knew about the Kellock book: Houdini, His Life and Times. It was a rare book in which Harry's widow, Bess Houdini, told the story — and the mythology — about her amazing husband. It went out of print in 1930, but of course, her father had a copy in his collection of magic books.

Pro turned to her computer and entered all the words she could think of in the search engine. "Kellock Houdini Code" got several hits, and one of them took her to the entire book online. She went through the scanned pages until she reached a familiar one with numbers listed for words. It read:

Pray   1

Answer	2
Say	3
Now	4
Tell	5
Please	6
Speak	7
Quickly	8
Look	9
Be Quick.	10

All the same words used in the message! No wonder the email couldn't be translated. It used the Houdini Code from more than a hundred years earlier. And only a magician would know where it was from or how to read it!

A magician…and her.

She printed up the page with the code, then set it side-by-side with the email page and set to work. She noted on the subject line that "Be Quick Twice Tell" was the first phrase before a hyphen. Well, if "Be Quick" equaled ten, twice would be the number twenty. Combine that with "Tell" which was the number five, and you had twenty-five.

She turned to the computer and did a search on "numbers equal letters code." The first entry was a code used by the Boy Scouts and listed it like this:

A	B	C	D	E	F	G	H	I	J	K	L	M	N
1	2	3	4	5	6	7	8	9	10	11	12	13	14

O	P	Q	R	S	T	U	V	W	X	Y	Z
15	16	17	18	19	20	21	22	23	24	25	26

She printed that page as well. Then she put it next to her other papers, and set to work. If "Be Quick Twice Tell" was indeed twenty-five, that would be the letter Y.

She assumed the hyphen was the break between letters, and that anything between hyphens was to be added together. She also decided that the commas represented the spaces between the entire words.

She worked away, and it was slow going, as she caught mistakes in her technique and had to refine it. However, about forty-five minutes later, she had this message handwritten across the paper with the email:

Subject: Your Fee

Message: The Fee is as we agreed. I will cut you in.

A smile came across Pro's face. Not only had she broken the code, she translated the message so that it made sense.

She glanced at the phone on her desk, wanting to call her partner, but realizing that perhaps a night with the auburn-haired Ms. Barker was exactly what he needed.

She glanced at the list of emails. She soon located and printed up the individual ones the Cyber Unit had sent to them between btg@magic.us and al@flossmagic.com.

As the printer made noise creating finished documents, Pro realized two things: she was famished, and her father had been right.

There was someone else involved who might indeed be the murderer.

And he was definitely a magician.

10. DeKolta Chair

P ro grabbed a greasy burger and even greasier fries at the bodega near the subway stop for her Brooklyn apartment. She carried her leather attaché under one arm and her purse under the other. Unwrapping the burger as she walked, she took bites of the meat and bread combination as she walked toward home. She made little humming noises of pleasure in the back of her throat as she went.

By the time she'd reached her brownstone, the burger was gone, and she wiped the grease from her hands with a wad of napkins as she got her key.

Once she was through the outer door, she headed up the three floors to her studio, munching on fries one at a time.

She undid the three locks on her door—two were deadbolts, and one that held a metal bar in place. The lock jammed the bar into a holder on the floor and made the door impossible to break through.

The joys of life in NYC.

She came in and dumped her things onto the coffee table in front of the sofa that was her pull-out bed. She stuffed another fry into her mouth as she headed toward her tiny kitchen, then paused. The sofa was closed, and she was sure she left it open and her bed a mess when she headed out to get coffee for her mother that morning. Now it was closed and there was even the blanket she used on chilly nights, neatly folded on top.

She glanced around the room. There certainly was hardly any place to hide. There was only the one room, taken up by the sofa and the coffee table, with two chairs just beyond the reach of the open bed. One padded chair covered with cloth, and the other one was a director's chair that she could fold up to make more room. Then she had her bathroom with its shower, and a little kitchen that was more of an alcove.

There was, however, a large closet, and the door was closed. Her hand went automatically to her service weapon under her jacket. She pulled it out and took it into a two-handed grip.

"I don't think you want to do that, pumpkin."

Pro spun, her weapon extended in a shooter's stance as she faced her father, who stepped out of the kitchenette with his empty hands raised in surrender.

"Max, for chrissakes!" Pro hissed and lowered her weapon. She put on the safety and jammed it back into her holster. "You need to turn yourself in."

"I will, I will, but right now you need me!"

"Max, you escaped from a holding cell! That is a big deal! They put out an APB on you. I could lose my shield just talking to you."

"I can't help you if I'm locked up, honey."

"Don't you dare call me 'honey.' My name is Pro — Pro Thompson."

Max held up his hands defensively. "Okay, Pro. But don't you want to know what I found out since I've been out?"

"No, I want you to sit in a chair while I call for backup."

"Pro, you gotta listen to me. The killer is still out there, and I think other people could end up dead."

"All the more reason you should be in a nice cell," Pro said pointing a finger at her father. "To prove you are not the one who is committing these murders!"

"Word on the street is that the plans for Prism are still for sale out there. I even heard that there might be a prototype."

"Do you know who might be any of the interested buyers or the next target?"

"I went to see Sam Lovell of Lovell Magic. He gave me the name of two other guys besides Shaut."

Pro reached into her attaché and pulled out her detective notebook. "Give!"

"Adrian Novack, who goes by Adrianna Gray. She's a female magician with a touring stage show. She's been trying to rip off parts of my act for years."

"Could she come up with the fifty grand that Shaut was talking about?"

"Hard to say. The other name he gave me was Michael Mystique."

"Isn't he one of those guys in a comic book?"

Max sighed. "Don't blame me. I didn't give them their stage names."

"Says Max Marvell!"

"Okay, point taken. They might have information that could help lead you to the killer."

Pro finished writing and put down her notebook with an angry sigh. "Okay, I'm going to share something with you — I don't know why!"

"What is it?"

She reached into her attaché and pulled out one of the coded emails, which she had not yet translated.

"What is this?" Max asked as she handed him a printout.

"Look at it. What does that look like to you?"

Max studied the paper for a moment. "That's the Houdini code."

Pro smiled. "I know."

"What?"

Pro reached into the attaché and pulled out the email with the notes she had written. "I translated it," she added triumphantly.

Max took the paper, gave it a once-over, and gave a smile of pride. "You sure did! This is good work, Pro."

"I am a detective."

"How did you figure it out?"

"Because of you. I remembered when I was little and saw the mentalists at A Night of Wonder and thought they were real. You told me how the trick worked and showed me the Kellock Houdini."

Max frowned. "You were barely five years old…"

"I know, but it all came back to me, and I found the book online and find the page with the code."

"And then you just figured everything else out," Max said. "Wow! I have a really smart daughter."

He raised his hand and wiped his eye as Pro stood in amazement.

"Are you… crying, Max?"

"Just something in my eye," Max said and blinked rapidly. "Kid, between the two of us, we could figure this case out."

"Max…" Pro lowered her voice. "I am serious. Turn yourself in. I'll call my partner. We can escort you to the precinct, make sure no one gets hurt."

"I can't do that, Pro. Two people are dead because of my invention. I have to stop the killer."

"Right now, there are people who think *you* are the killer. Max, there is an APB out on you. Somebody might shoot first and ask questions later."

"I'm good at hiding."

"Max… Dad," Pro pleaded, and Max looked at her in surprise. "Dad, I don't want you to end up dead."

Tears flashed in Max's eyes. "Well, that's a step in the right direction."

"So sit down, let me call my partner, and I can still have a father, okay?"

A tear fell from Max's left eye. "Okay, pumpkin, you're right. I went too far."

He walked over to the padded chair and sat down with his back to Pro. "Okay, call!"

Keeping her eyes on Max, she went to the kitchenette and pulled out her cell. In moments it was ringing, and Chu picked up.

"Can't I get a night off?" he said, annoyed.

"Tom, I have Max at my apartment."

"What? How did he get there?"

"I'm still trying to figure out how he got my address," Pro said, and looked at the chair. She hadn't turned on many lights when she came in, but could see Max's silhouette plainly.

"Wait! He broke into your apartment?"

"More likely picked the locks. He's very good at that."

"I know."

"I made a deal with him to escort him back to the precinct. But obviously I need him to be driven over. I can't just take him by subway."

"Christ! Hold on," Chu said, and then it sounded like he spoke to someone with his hand over the microphone of the phone. "Okay, I can be on the road in ten minutes. Thank God I'm dating someone who knows the job."

A female voice said something indistinct, and she heard Tom say, "She knows…I don't know how, she figured it out…I don't know, radar or something!"

Another burst of indistinct babbling, with a conciliatory tone, and Tom was back. "Okay, I'm heading out there. You keep an eye on him."

She looked over. "I'm watching him right now, Tom. See you soon."

She hung up the phone and went through the doorway to start the kettle. "You want coffee, Max? It's not very good, but it's strong."

No answer.

She stuck her head back in the room and saw Max's silhouette in the same place in the chair. "What happened? Cat got your tongue?"

She walked over to the chair, but it was empty. Attached to the top of the chair was a cardboard cutout of Max's silhouette. She touched it and it fell over on a makeshift hinge.

A realization hit her, and she ran to the table with her attaché case. The papers with all the coded messages were gone.

She ran over to the front door, yanked it open, and headed to the stairs.

"You goddamn old bastard!" she screamed looking down.

A door opened on the floor below her. "Hey, shut the hell up!"

"Sorry," Pro snapped, but shot her middle finger at the unknown complainer before she went back into her apartment.

"What do you mean, gone?" Chu demanded.

They were in her studio apartment, and Pro led him to the gimmicked chair to show him the fake silhouette. "Honestly, I don't know how he could have done it. I only looked away to hit your number on my phone."

"You couldn't call me when I was en route?"

"I thought you should see how he fooled me."

Chu blew out his breath in a steady stream, like a deflating balloon. "He fooled you because he knows how to push your buttons. Like any magician, he gets you to look where he wants you to look to trick you."

Pro glanced down, embarrassed. "You're right. And God, he snuck into my apartment like he freakin' owned the place!"

"You could press charges." Tom said with a grin.

"If I thought for a minute that it would make him act sensibly, I would. He stole the emails I printed up, but I cracked the code."

"The code?" Tom repeated.

"Yeah, in those weird emails with all the 'Answer-Pray' stuff. It's an alphanumeric code based on an act Houdini did with his wife."

Chu considered this. "Did Max tell you that?"

Pro shook her head. "No, I figured it out myself. But now, I'll have to print up the papers again."

"Leave it go until tomorrow, Pro, but I fully expect we are both working on Sunday."

"We were supposed to be off, but until this case is closed and Max placed where we can find him—"

"See you about ten in the morning," Chu said as he neared the door.

"Sorry about your date," she apologized.

"You should be. It looked like tonight was going to be the night," Chu grumbled.

"Sorry," Pro sympathized. "Now I really feel bad."

"Well, we want to try for an actual relationship, so there will be other chances. Good night, Pro."

"'Night, Tom," she said and shut the door after him.

She moved to her tiny kitchen and opened the door of the refrigerator. It wasn't close to being as tall as her, coming only up to her chest. Extracting a large bottle of white wine, she grabbed a jelly jar from the dish rack and filled it full of wine. She drank half the glass in one shot. She refilled the jar, put the cork back into the wine, and returned the bottle to the fridge.

She walked to the other room, took off her jacket, and hung it in her small closet. She moved the seat cushions and pulled the frame to unfold the bed.

When she opened it, sitting atop the neatly folded sheets, a red sponge was there. Pro reached down and touched it. It was a little smaller than her hand, and the shape was an outline of a rabbit.

Her father had done this when she was little, hidden sponge rabbits in her things. Sometimes in her bed, sometimes in her shoe—all different places. When she was little, she asked why he did it.

"Because I love you, pumpkin, and when you see the rabbit, it reminds you I do."

She couldn't help but smile, then shook her head in amazement that he was still trying to influence her after what he'd just pulled.

Removing her service weapon and taking off her harness, she hung the harness from the closet rod. She picked up the locking metal box and set the three small dials on the correct numbers. Once the box was open, she placed it on the bed, then quickly made sure the pistol's chamber was empty, then pulled the magazine. She went to place the magazine in the box when she saw a piece of paper.

Frowning, she pulled the paper out. Scrawled on it was this:

> Sorry for the trouble.
>
> I really do love you.
>
> MAX

She shook her head and grabbed the glass of wine to take another sip. "How the hell did he get into this box?"

11. Botania

The next morning, Pro was walking with coffee up West End Avenue toward her mother's apartment.

She'd decided when she woke up that if Max was still going to be in touch with anyone, it would be his ex-wife.

And despite Elisha telling her they had a fight, she might cover for him. She wanted to lay down the law, so that if Max showed up at her mother's door, Elisha would call the police.

She went up the elevator and considered her arguments. They needed to be strong, to let her mother know in no uncertain terms that aiding or abetting her ex-husband could mean that charges would come down upon her head. Not to mention the fact that her NYPD detective daughter could lose her job.

She unlocked the door and picked up the cups of coffee and walked in with a yell of "MOMMA?"

To a garden.

At least that is how it appeared at first glance. It seemed like flowers covered every spot. A sea of different blooms covered piece of furniture held in vases of various sizes. The table she had sat at the previous day seemed to bend from the assorted greenery placed on it.

The only way to move about the apartment was through a narrow path in the middle of the room that allowed her access to the bedroom.

She placed the cups in a tiny space open on the table that barely fit the pair and knocked carefully on the bedroom door. "Momma? Are you alone?"

"Oh come on in, sweetie, it's all right."

She opened the door and was relieved that the flora did not continue to this section of the living quarters. Her mother was in a robe and was standing up next to the bed.

She indicated the flowers. "What is all this? Who did this?"

Elisha smiled. "It was your father." She stepped to a nearby desk and grabbed a large cardboard heart and offered it to Pro to read.

Pro opened the card to reveal a hand-written message in her father's firm hand:

Elisha

I am an insensitive jerk.

Please forgive me.

I would like to see you again.

Max

"Well, I agree with the insensitive jerk part," Pro admitted. "Have you seen him?"

"Since yesterday?"

"Well, he spent the previous night in your bed."

"Oh, will you let it go!" Elisha sighed and strode past her daughter toward the door. "You better've brought me coffee if you gonna interrogate me this early in the day."

Pro followed her mother into the other room. She had to admit that it really smelled wonderful, with all the exotic floral scents. Though there was hardly a place to sit or put anything down.

"How did he even do this?"

"I don't know. I went shopping and came home to this. The card was on the floor as I came in. Some chocolates, too."

Pro froze. "You have chocolate? Good chocolate?"

"I saved you some," Elisha grumbled. "The box is on the table."

"I can't see anything but the flowers and the coffee I brought," Pro said while getting on tiptoe to peer around the miniature forest.

"Well, give me my coffee and I'll find the chocolates for you."

Pro handed her mother a cup, and she took a grateful sip.

Elisha reached past a rhododendron and extracted a medium-sized, half-empty, open box of chocolates. Each one was a perfect sphere dusted with fine cocoa powder. She held it out for her daughter, who took one and popped it into her mouth.

"Wow, that's good," Pro moaned, her eyes closed as she savored the dark sweetness that made her knees weak.

Her mother raised an eyebrow. "Max knows how to get to my heart."

"Yes, Mother," Pro retorted. "And how to get into your pants."

Elisha put on a smug smile. "I guess so or you wouldn't be here."

"Seriously, Mother. How did all this get here? Did he break in? And with the APB out, they've frozen Max's credit cards. How did he pay for all this?"

"I don't have an answer for you, baby."

Pro grabbed another piece of chocolate. "He was in my apartment last night."

"What?"

"There waiting for me. He made my bed."

"The nerve." Elisha grinned.

"It's not funny, Mom. It's disconcerting that he can sneak flowers into your place and just show up in mine."

"Did you arrest him?"

"I thought I persuaded him to turn himself in. Then he disappeared and took some evidence I had brought home."

Elisha tried to look serious, but as her daughter went on, her mouth twitched and a chuckle escaped her lips.

"Mother, it's not funny! He left me a sponge rabbit and a note that told me he loved me!"

This broke Elisha's resistance, and a loud guffaw burst from her. She doubled over with laughter as Pro continued to protest.

"Mother, you have got to take this seriously! This is a police investigation… of a murder."

By this time, Elisha had pulled out a chair from the overburdened table and sat down as she continued to be swept away by waves of merriment.

This frustrated Pro and she walked over to her stepfather's favorite easy chair, which now held a potted palm tree. She removed the small arboreal, got her coffee, and sat down as her mother continued to be helpless with glee.

Finally, after a couple of minutes, Elisha had laughed herself out and calmed down. She pulled a napkin from somewhere in the bower and daubed her eyes and blew her nose.

"I should eat all of your chocolate to punish you for laughing at me," Pro sniped from her chair.

This got another giggle from her mother, who held out the box. "Knock yourself out, baby girl."

She grudgingly came over, took several candies, and ate them one at a time between swigs of coffee. "I feel like I did when I was a kid."

"What do you mean, honey?"

"I mean all the craziness around Max. I didn't have any idea what was going on and didn't understand half of it."

"Honey, you were a child. There's nothing you could've done."

Pro leaned forward. "Well, I'm not a child now, but he's treating me like one. Showing up at my place, breaking in here to deliver flowers. We're not safe."

"Max is trying to help… in his way," Elisha explained.

Pro shook her head. "It's a damn annoying way. If he knows something, he should just tell me — tell us."

"Your father has spent his life keeping and creating secrets. You have to understand how hard it is for him to open up. And I have to admit, I didn't help."

"Mom, Max left you. I don't see how you could blame yourself."

Elisha bit her lip. "I guess I told you that because I wanted it to be easy. I wanted it to be simple for you."

"What do you mean, Mom?"

"Max wanted to take us to Vegas with him. He wanted to buy us a house and be a family there."

Pro frowned. "No, he left us…"

"Temporarily, honey. He asked me to go. Promised that within a year he'd buy us a house."

Pro looked at her mother, overcome with the feeling that everything in her world had just tipped off-center. "I don't understand."

"I was afraid!" Elisha snapped. "Afraid that if I gave up my job as a designer, I wouldn't find one out there. I figured if I lost my job and his show wasn't a success, we'd be stuck in Vegas and be flat broke."

Elisha turned from her daughter and looked at the flowers as she sipped her coffee. "But it's not what happened. Max became big, bigger than he ever planned. But then it was too late. I had filed for divorce and I made my commitment to stay here in New York."

Elisha turned back and Pro could see tears in her eyes. "So, I lied to you. I told you Max left us, but that wasn't totally true. I wouldn't follow him, I wouldn't trust him, probably when he needed me the most." Tears fell as Elisha lowered her head. "I was afraid…"

Pro rose from the chair and knelt in front of her mother, taking the older woman's hands in her own. "Now you listen to me. You were the finest mother anyone could have asked for."

But now Elisha was sobbing. "You hated your father all these years because I lied to you. You thought he didn't care. He wanted to come back to New York, just to be with you, but I told him no."

"Momma, you did the best you could…"

"You wanted to know why I defended him, why I said nothing bad? It was 'cause I knew the truth. I let you blame him and that was wrong…"

"Momma…"

"I'm sorry, honey. If it wasn't for Joe, I don't know what we would've done."

She raised her mother's tear-streaked face to meet her eyes. "You did good. And Joe did good. You loved me and raised me. But Max is the problem right now. He's a fugitive and he might get himself shot… or worse."

"What can I do?" Elisha sniffled.

"Call me or the police if he gets in touch at all. Locks seem to be no impediment to him, so keep aware that he might be back."

Elisha nodded and grabbed another napkin to wipe her nose. "Okay, honey, I will."

"I love you, Momma."

"I love you too, baby. Please don't shoot your father."

"I'll try not to," Pro said and rose to her feet. Her mother stood as well and hugged her daughter fiercely.

"Now, go find the actual killer, because I know it is not your father."

12. Signed Card

B ack in the Midtown North Precinct, Pro had reprinted the select coded emails and was halfway through translating them as Chu entered the bullpen.

"You got an early start," Tom said as he sat at his desk.

"Had a heart-to-heart with my mom. By the way, Max visited her house yesterday and delivered about a gazillion flowers."

Chu shook his head. "Honestly, forget superheroes. This guy can do anything."

"Don't attribute supernatural powers to him just yet. I let Max glance at the emails yesterday to see if I was right about the Houdini code."

"Maybe you should have handcuffed him to a table."

"Tom, he left me a note in my pistol lock box! He picked the lock on a holding cell. You really think handcuffs are a challenge to him?"

"Okay, okay," Chu relented. "So, what was your point?"

"Max has a photographic memory. I think when he saw those papers, he translated them in his head. He saw something that pushed him to take them. I think Max's next move is going to be based on something in those coded emails."

"And what do you propose?" Chu asked skeptically.

"Well, I've decoded about half of them. Mostly they are brief messages about the fact that the 'btg@magic.us' guy had worked out the techniques behind 'Prism.' He was looking for a front man to do the deal, and he would split the take."

"Okay, if you keep converting the messages, I'll try to track down the emails of the buyers to find out who they are."

"I also need you to track down these guys," Pro added, and pulled a page from her detective notebook.

Chu read the paper aloud. "Adrian Novack, aka Adrianna Gray, and Michael Mystique. Who are they?"

"Magicians and potential buyers. Which means Max might go to visit one or both of them."

"I'll get started on those names first."

"Also a Sam Lovell of Lovell Magic. Max talked to him yesterday, so he might know where Max is hiding."

"Got it!" Chu moved to his computer to look up the names on the internet.

Pro didn't want to admit that, so far, there didn't seem to be all that much from the transcribed emails. There was one that gave the time and place for a meeting that had been last week, so it wasn't much help. The rest were discussions of price in the terse messages.

She pulled up the next one and started on the subject line.

Chu cleared his throat. "I have a Lovell Magic on West 73rd Street."

Pro shook her head. "How many freakin' magic shops are in this town?"

"Never thought about it. By the way, that's 20th precinct, so I'm going to put in a courtesy call to let them know that we're in their neck of the woods."

"Okay," Pro agreed and moved to the message, turning the words into numbers, the numbers into letters, and finally back into words.

In the meantime, Chu used his desk phone and spoke to a detective he knew at the 20th. He asked about family and mutual acquaintances, then explained that he and his partner would question a witness in their jurisdiction. He also asked if the detective had the APB on Max Martin, aka Marvell.

As he hung up the phone, Pro was finishing up the email.

"Tom," Pro called out, head still leaned over the paper she was writing on. "Any luck with Adrianna Gray?"

"No, I was about to do a search."

"Well, do it quickly. She's mentioned in the message here."

"What does it say?"

"Best as I've done, it reads like this: 'Gray might win by many yards. See who is still in the tip.'"

"What was it, a race? And what tip?"

Pro sat back in her chair and looked at the ceiling. "It sounds like 'Carny.'"

"What?"

"In the beginning of his career, Max worked carnivals—"

"Here we go," Chu growled.

"Will you listen?" Pro demanded. "Even after I was born, Max would sometimes use Carney lingo, shorthand expressions that carnival workers use, like the ones we use."

"What's your point?"

"Well, 'yard' is a hundred dollars, so Gray winning by many yards means she offered more money. 'Tip' is carny for a crowd, so 'See who is still in the tip' refers to the other buyers."

Chu folded his arms. "It appears your father was giving you an education without you even knowing it."

Pro looked down at the marked-up paper. "I guess so."

"Okay, I found an address for Adrian Novak, and it's just south of our magic store on 73rd."

"Let's hit the store first. So far, our dead magicians had stores." Pro grabbed her papers, shoved them into her attaché, and headed out right behind Chu.

They arrived at Broadway and 73rd Street, and Chu parked in front of a hydrant. In the car's windshield, he put out their laminated sign that read "POLICE ON DUTY."

Pro looked up at the eighteen-story Beaux-Art style structure. The designers gave it striking architectural features and round turrets on the corners that faced Broadway.

"This is the Ansonia," Pro said.

"I guess. What of it?" Chu asked.

"I've just always admired the architecture. I used to walk by the building. It always seemed like a fairy castle that got dropped in the Upper West Side."

"Well, our magic store is inside somewhere on the first floor," Chu said as he headed for a nearby elaborate door with a green awning that stated: The Ansonia.

They stepped into a hallway; the floors done in elaborate black-and-white marble tile. At the entrance was black veined marble on both walls with lighting sconces in the shape of elaborate seashells. As they moved in, among the white woodwork and wainscoting were doorways for businesses on each side of the hall. Each door had a small, tasteful sign, and since it was the same for each door, it was apparently a requirement that you buy signs from a specific vendor.

As the pair continued toward the main lobby, a brightly lit area in the center, they passed a door on their left which read, "Ansonia Realty."

"Hold on," Chu said and tried the doorknob to the office. It turned and allowed them into a tiny waiting room, which held only a small desk with a smiling salesperson and two chairs opposite. She was a blonde woman, not young, perhaps forty-five or fifty. She wore a black turtleneck and a white sports coat. Gold earrings hung from her ears, and she had a pair of horn-rimmed glasses on the desk, where it looked like she put them when the door opened.

"How can I help you?" the blonde asked in an attempt to sound perky. "Interested in looking at a condo today?"

Both detectives opened their billfolds in one practiced move.

"NYPD," Chu said, his voice suddenly deeper. "We want to know where the Lovell Magic Shop is located."

"Oh dear, is Mister Lovell in any kind of trouble?"

Pro cleared her throat. "We just need to ask him some questions."

She didn't rise from behind her desk. "Oh, okay. Well, you just go through the main lobby and straight down the hallway opposite and it's there."

"Thank you," Chu said. "By the way, have there been any complaints about Mister Lovell, or anything we should know about?"

"Oh no, he's a very good tenant." The blonde's big smile returned. "He's really interested in the building's history."

"How do you mean?" Pro inquired.

"Well, he's always asking to look at the blueprints. He says he loves to tell people about the past, with scandals and the good stuff, too! We had some people interested in condos after talking to him."

"Really?" Pro said. "You keep copies of the blueprints here?"

"Sure, in our files. We have copies of the original blueprints from 1899—those are really old. Then we have blueprints of all the units during the renovations. Those come in handy when people want to see the unit they're interested in. Mister Lovell looks at both sets, because he wants to find the apartment Babe Ruth lived in."

"So you like Mister Lovell?" Pro pushed.

"Sure, every time he comes here, he shows me a magic trick. He's really good!"

"Thank you for your time, Miss—"

"Edmonds, Cathy Edmonds," the woman said. She picked up a small piece of cardboard off her desk and handed it to Pro. "Here's my card, in case you're ever interested in a condo…"

Pro smiled. "Probably out of my price range."

"We rent some apartments as well. There's nothing like living in a piece of New York history!"

Chu and Pro both smiled and waved as they went back into the hall. They continued their journey, and in a few hundred feet, they were suddenly in the elaborate open lobby. The floor tiles shifted to tan and black, and the ceiling rose several stories. There was a large carpet over a center space, and an enormous chandelier provided illumination. The sitting area had two back-to-back sofas, a pair of coffee tables, and leather wingback chairs on each of the carpet's four corners.

"Not bad," Chu said, looking at the white woodwork and the faux windows, which were filled with multiple panes of cut glass with elaborate curved tops on each one.

They continued down a hall across from where they had entered, which also had doors on both sides. The tile on the floor shifted back to black-and-white marble, and halfway to the exit, a door on the left caught Pro's eye.

"Here we go," Pro said, pointing at the sign for "Lovell's Magic."

Chu opened the door and stepped in as an automatic bell announced their entrance. The shop was small but spotless, with only two display cases.

Props sat on a single bookcase against the wall that faced the door. A thin man with long, unkempt hair and glasses with a thick frame came out.

"Can I 'elp you folks?" he said with a British accent that sounded cockney.

Once again, the detectives showed their shields.

"Ah! 'ow can I 'elp the NYPD today? Maybe some tips on catching a card cheat?"

"Are you Sam Lovell?" Chu said.

"Indeed, I am," he replied as he pushed his glasses farther back on his nose with his pinky.

"Max Marvell," Pro demanded, as Chu extracted a print of the mug shot taken while Max had been in police custody. "We are looking for him."

"'Ave you tried in Vegas? Last time, I 'eard that's where—"

Pro interrupted, "Don't be coy, Mister Lovell. We know Max came to see you within the last twenty-four hours."

Chu took over. "Max Martin, aka Max Marvell, escaped from NYPD custody. If you have assisted him, we can bring you up on charges of aiding a fugitive. Those are serious charges."

Lovell riveted his eyes on Pro's face and spoke up when she returned his stare. "You're Prophecy, aren't you? Your blue eyes gave it away. They're so striking."

Pro nodded, her mouth a thin line. "Yes, I am. Now please answer the question. Have you seen Max Marvell?"

"He came by yesterday, right when I was closing up. Said 'e needed 'elp, and that he was tracking down the person who stole his 'Prism' effect. Told me someone murdered old Al Floss. Is that true?"

Pro sighed. "Yes, it is. Did he ask you about any buyers trying to get their hands on the trick?"

"That 'e did. I told 'im Adrianna Gray and Mike Mystique were both in the market from what I 'eard. I was interested meself but bowed out when the price got too 'igh."

"Why?" Chu interjected, his notebook in his hands.

"'Cause it's amazing. I saw the video online. Man, you want to talk about an ending…"

"We haven't seen it," Pro stated flatly.

"Really?" Lovell exclaimed. "Stay right 'ere. I'll get me laptop."

He wandered through a curtain, and Pro wondered why all the magic shops had a curtain between storage and retail? What was wrong with a freakin' door?

A moment later, Lovell came out with a laptop in his hand. He placed the device on the counter, turned it to face the detectives, and pulled up a video.

"I downloaded it so I could watch it over and over," Lovell divulged. "Someone shot it with a cell phone, because it is the only footage of the effect ever smuggled out."

He hit the space bar on the computer, and the video played.

It was Max on stage, looking like the classic magician in black tails with a white vest. He carried a black walking stick as he entered to the applause from the audience.

"This is 'is finalé," Lovell explained. "He's done the full show, and this is 'ow he ends it."

Max acknowledged the audience, and the live orchestra ceased playing. Max spoke, his booming voice carried and amplified throughout the room. "I have one last effect I want to share with you. I have to tell you, it is unlike anything you've ever seen. I would like to say it is the closest thing I have ever done to real magic."

As he paused, the curtain behind him went up. On the stage were two large, triangular crystals standing upright on top of two revolving platforms. They flashed and caught the stage lights in the depths of the glass.

The orchestra played quietly as Max stepped back and moved one of the platforms to a specific location on the stage. It slid easily on wheels. With a touch to a foot pedal, it locked in place. As a flute played a solo with a wistful tune, he rolled the other to its proper place.

"For centuries, magicians have been able to disappear with the use of mirrors, black curtains, and trapdoors," Max spoke over the music. The beige microphone that hung off his ear amplified his voice. "We will have none of that here!"

With a gesture, as the music grew in speed and volume, the back curtain rose. This revealed the plain brick of the theater's back wall, which was a respectful distance from Max.

"You could fit a plane on that stage," Chu whispered.

"Max did, five years ago," Lovell corrected. "But watch."

On the video, Max moved to the center of the stage, where he was in plain view. The light grew brighter, making the lit figure of Max the most prominent feature.

They cut the spotlight on Max, as there was enough stage light to see him easily.

"Ladies and gentlemen, thank you for sharing your evening with me and my humble illusions. For my finalé — an effect I call Prism."

He waved at one of the upstanding crystals, and it spun faster. He gestured at the other dramatically, and it did the same.

"Watch closely," Max cautioned. "Don't look away!"

He held the walking stick aloft, made a circle in front of himself with it…

And was gone.

There was no explosion or pyrotechnics, no cloth to hide behind.

Max merely disappeared.

The orchestra hit a crescendo and ceased playing. The empty stage and silence of the vast audience was astounding. Then the entire stage went to black.

As the audience applauded and cheered, the lights came on again, and Max stood with the entire company of the singers, dancers, and assistants as they all took a bow.

Lovell hit the space bar, and the image froze. "What did I tell you, eh?"

"That's not possible," Chu insisted. "It had to be a camera trick. He's not really there. It's a projection or something."

Lovell shook his head. "Nice guess, detective. I like the way your mind works. But no, it's what you just saw. No trapdoor, no smoke, no mirrors, nothing. 'E's there and then 'e's gone."

"I can see why magicians would want this," Pro marveled.

"Yeah, and I 'eard 'e did it at a lecture in Vegas on a freakin' platform. So, it doesn't even need a large stage."

"Back to the work at hand," Chu broke in. "Do you know where Max is or how to get in touch with him?"

"Not really," Lovell considered. "But 'e stopped by again this morning and left something with me. Said 'e'd pick it up or his daughter Prophecy would be by and I could give it to 'er."

He again stepped out of the room and came back with a small box, about the right size to hold stationary. He offered it to Pro.

Pro pulled the box open. In it were a smartphone and several credit and debit cards. They rested on top of the papers Max had purloined from his daughter's attaché case the previous evening.

"When did he give this to you?" Pro questioned.

"This morning. I opened at 10:00, and 'e was on me doorstep. 'E said this was important."

"While we are here, Mister Lovell, can you tell us your whereabouts on Friday morning at 10:00 AM?"

"I was in a meetin'."

"Anyone to corroborate this?"

"I should say so. Ten people, in fact. It was at the Rutger's Church. I was attending an AA meeting."

"Alcoholics Anonymous?" Chu pressed.

Lovell nodded. "I'll give you the name of me sponsor, if you like."

"Please," said Chu as he took a pen to his notebook. Lovell rattled it off, along with a telephone number.

"Thank you, Mister Lovell," Chu said.

Pro chimed in. "Unless you have anything else you want to tell us. I mean, I'd like to know how you knew Ms. Gray and Mister Mystique were looking into Prism."

Lovell shrugged. "I keep me ear to the ground. It's a tight community, and when things 'appen, we all know. That's 'ow I knew about poor Al."

"I take it you don't think Max killed him?"

"Max? Kill Al? Neveh!"

Pro and Chu exchanged a look.

"Max might've been angry, maybe said a few things 'e didn't mean, but Max wouldn't 'urt Al. Not ever!"

13. Fire Wallet

- -

Fifteen minutes later, Chu and Pro headed up
the steps of a brownstone on 70th Street
between Amsterdam and West End Avenue.

"Anything on the phone that can help?" Chu
asked.

"No, it's pass-coded, so I can't open it. However,
the last missed call was from my mother. I recognize
the number."

"At least she tried to get in touch with him," Chu
pointed out.

"I asked her to convince him to surrender," Pro
said. "Any reports about Max? Have they spotted
him at all?"

"It appears Max Marvell is quite good at covering
his tracks. And with his phone tucked away at
Lovell's store, we couldn't even track him down with
that if we'd gotten the chance."

At the top of the short flight of stairs, built into
the brick wall, was a metal plate with several white
buttons. Chu pushed the one with a label marked

"Novack" as Pro put the box with the cell phone in her attaché.

There was a loud buzz, and the detectives opened the door and entered the building.

"The buzzer said 1-D," Chu stated.

"At least we're not doing stairs," Pro said as they reached the door with a brass "1-D" screwed to the front.

Chu knocked on the door.

"Who is it?" came the reply.

"NYPD, ma'am. We need to talk to you about Albert Floss."

The door opened abruptly, and an average-height woman with a wild mass of blonde hair stood in the doorway. She was at least fifty, though her body was curvaceous from workouts and possible surgical augmentation. She was wearing a leopard-spotted cat suit, and Pro couldn't help but wonder how she got out of it when she needed to pee.

She wore the scent of scotch and sweat.

"Come in, detectives. Please show me your badges."

"Shields, Miss Novack," Pro countered as she opened her billfold. "Detectives have shields."

The woman pushed her hair to one side to better see the identification. "You guys want a drink? It's Sunday, and I'm off, so I'm drinking."

It appeared to Pro that Miss Novack started imbibing early in the day and was very far ahead of any visitors who might drop by.

"No, ma'am," Chu said.

"Do I look like a 'ma'am' to you?" Adrian said, and stood up straight so that her impressive chest thrust out at Chu, who stepped back a bit in surprise. Adrian considered it for a moment, then relaxed, turned and walked back toward a sofa. "Yeah, I guess I do."

She sat down languidly and picked up a nearby cocktail and took a delicate sip, which made the half-melted ice cubes clink. "So how can I help you ossifers — officers?"

She smiled sweetly at them.

"Are you familiar with Al Floss?"

"I should be. He grabbed my ass every time I went into that damn store of his. Ugh, what a lecher! Fortunately, I knew enough not to get stuck in that back room with him."

Chu took out his pad and a pen. "You're suggesting that Mister Floss liked the ladies?"

"I'm suggested that 'ole Flossy' was a perv who put his hands where they were unwanted. But I don't think they'd bring up charges, considering I was one of maybe three women who ever went into his establishment."

"So, there aren't many female magicians?" Pro suggested.

"Damn straight!" Adrian said. "And I don't blame them. If you wanna be a female magician, you got to do everything a male magician does, except backwards and in a dress. Tell you, if I could sing, I would've never taken it up."

"Really?" Pro said as a way of encouragement.

"Sure, can't carry a tune at all. And the other reason there aren't a lot of women in magic is that guys learn tricks to get laid! Not that most of them ever do. But a lady doesn't need illusions to get stud service. Ya get me, sweetie?" She gave Pro an overtly obvious wink.

Pro gave a wan smile, her coffee and cream complexion turning a tad red. "Sure, sure."

Chu cleared his throat. "Miss Novack—"

"I'm Gray," she corrected drunkenly. "Adrianna Gray."

She gestured at several posters on the wall that showed her in different, tight costumes. In one, she was holding a magician's top hat, from which came an endless supply of silks, flowers, and other paraphernalia. She wore a short set of tails with fishnet stockings, high heels, and a black thong.

The next poster showed her in a formal evening dress with a man floating horizontally in the air with only a broom supporting him under his one arm. He was the one wearing very little in this poster— just shorts and a bike messenger shirt.

The final poster had her in a bikini holding a rabbit high in the air and bore the caption, "NOTHING UP MY SLEEVES." It must have been from years earlier, because in the cat suit you could see where she had filled out a little more than in the advertisement.

"Miss... uh... Gray," Chu said. "I need to know where you were on Friday between 10:00 and 11:00 AM."

"Driving!" she moaned. "I was just getting back into town after a week of gigs in fuckin' Pennsylvania."

"Really?" Pro said.

"That old bastard, Max Marvell, is working Vegas, every night the same theater, easy-peasy. I gotta rent vans and schlep all my crap to fuckin' Pennsylvania. I'm tellin' you this business sucks."

"Were you aware of Mister Floss's death?"

"Yeah, he probably grabbed the wrong broad's ass," she cackled at her own remark and sat down again.

"We understand," Pro said, "that you were attempting to buy a set of plans from Mister Floss."

"I wanted to. I wanted to show Max that I was his equal in every way. Do you know the last time I was in Vegas I offered him a blow job if he'd tell me the secret to Prism? The old bastard turned me down!" she huffed. "His loss!"

She took another sip from the cocktail.

Pro looked down at the floor and kept her anger in check. "Miss Gray, we need to know if you had any luck in attempting to purchase those plans."

"Nah! Got too rich for my blood. I don't have an extra fifty K for just one trick. Hell, I built my entire show for less than that — not much less, I'll tell you."

Chu tried to keep her on track. "Have you seen or spoken to anyone about the trick or the plans since Mister Floss's death on Friday?"

She shook her head in a loose, inebriated way. "No, sir, defective... uh... I mean, detective."

Pro leaned close. "Have you been in touch with Max Marvell in the last forty-eight hours?"

"Max?" she said and tried to focus. "Why would Max try to contact me?" She considered it for a moment, then laughed. "Maybe he wants to collect on that blow job."

She fell into a fit of giggles, delighted in her drunken wit.

Pro shook her head in disgust and murmured to her partner, "This is a waste of time."

With a nod, Chu spoke loudly, "Miss Gray, thank you for your hospitality. I am leaving my card." He took a card from his wallet and placed it on the table. "If you think of anything else, please call me."

She rose unsteadily and headed for the door. "Okay, thanks for comin' by." She opened it wide, and the detectives stepped out. "I'm gonna take a little nap."

"That might be a good idea," Chu said as the door closed.

"What a freakin' waste of time," Pro said. "Man, the mouth on her."

"She'll pay for it tomorrow, I'll bet," Chu said as they walked out to the street.

Back in the apartment, Adrian listened at the intercom as the detectives went down the stairs, then released the button and stood on her feet easily.

She pushed her hair out of her face and walked over to the large bookcase, and knocked on it twice. There was the sound of a release mechanism, and the bookcase opened up to reveal the small hidden room.

Max Marvell stepped out.

"They're gone," she told him, stone-cold sober. "And I gotta wash the stink of the scotch off me."

"Thank you, Adrianna," Max said and took her hands. "You were brilliant, an epic performance. I believed you were blotto myself."

"You taught me it's all in the misdirection," she said, and reached up to unclip the unruly hairpiece from her well-coifed hair. "Give them one thing to focus on and they won't look for another."

"I've never seen it done better."

"Thank you, sir. I hope you didn't mind the jabs aimed at you."

"Perfect choice. When you mentioned offering oral sex to me, I almost expected Prophecy's head to explode."

""She's a looker, your kid," Adrian said, as she poured out her soda with no alcohol and tidied up the room, designed to reinforce her drunken performance. "I'm always amazed that you had time to have a kid. I never could get that together."

Max paused and looked at the floor, dejected. "I was a terrible father…"

"Oh, you're just saying that—"

"No, I mean it. I wasn't there for her, and I should have been. But I guess I can only move forward from where I am."

"I'll get you a coffee and you can head out. Best to make sure they aren't scouring the neighborhood before you go."

Max stood in the living room alone, then turned and closed the open bookcase.

Michael Mystique's address was down on 51st Street, not a long drive from 73rd Street.

"So, apparently, this guy legally changed his name to Mystique," Chu offered to get Pro to stop brooding.

"That horrible woman," Pro muttered, and then changed her voice to imitate her. "'I offered him a blow job, but he turned me down.'"

"Pretty good impression."

"Nice to know I have drunken slut in my voice skill set. Never know where that's going to come in handy."

"She really didn't seem to care for Max."

"And he didn't take her up on her offer. I'm surprised. Between his multiple wives and numerous assistants, I figured he took any sexual favor ever offered him. Christ, my mom slept with that horny old bastard."

"Getting angry will not help our investigation."

"Sorry," Pro fretted. "No one knows where he is or what he's doing? We got three leads today, and two of them knew nothing."

"But at least we saw the video of the trick," Chu said, and then stole a glance at his partner. "Okay, tell me."

"Tell you what?"

"How does he do it?"

This made Pro grin. "I have absolutely no idea."

"You're kidding!"

"I don't know how magic tricks work because of my DNA. It looked impossible to me, too."

"Yes, and on an empty stage? It's gotta be a trapdoor."

"You heard what Shaut told us. He said he looked for one in the second show — no luck."

"Maybe Michael Mystique can shed some light on it?"

"Whatever," Pro said as Chu pulled the car into a parking space.

They got out and headed to a large apartment complex that was painted white and went up many stories. They headed into the lobby, which was also white, even the couches and pots for plants. Behind a large white desk, two men sat in security guard uniforms — those, at least, were blue. Pro and Chu flipped open their billfolds, and the men stood.

"How can we help, detectives?" the man on the left asked. He was a tall African-American man with a shaved head and the body of a linebacker.

Chu told them, "I need to see Mister Mystique in 12-C. Have you seen him today?"

"Not today," the skinny man on the right told them. He was a Hispanic man with a slight tinge to his skin, but absolutely no accent.

The bald man held out two visitor badges to Chu and Pro. "These will let you up the elevators. You can press Mister Mystique's buzzer when you reach his door."

"That will be the left elevator bank," the skinny man said and pointed in the correct direction.

Chu started off and Pro turned to say, "Thank you, gentlemen."

"And, detective," the bald black man said, which caught Pro's attention. "If you need anything, anything at all, just let me know. Here is the direct line to this desk."

He handed her a card, and Pro smiled as she caught the look in his eyes. "Thank you."

She headed to the elevator and felt giddy. Had it been so long since a man had watched her with a combination of admiration and lust that it gave her butterflies? Or was it the fact that he was definitely her type? Muscles, a handsome face, and a regard for law enforcement that was lacking in many places nowadays. He had treated her with total respect, but his eyes told her how much he wanted her. That combination of esteem and desire was a total aphrodisiac for Pro.

She took a deep breath and got into the elevator with her partner, focused on the job at hand. But maybe on the way out she could give the handsome guard her card, instead of Chu.

Did she need another complication in her life? Relationships were a pain, and between her mother and her estranged father, did she have the time or energy to give to another person?

The door slid open, and they walked out to the hall and over to the apartment marked 12-C.

It had an intercom with a button right next to the door, with a nameplate that read "M. MYSTIQUE."

Chu pressed the button and waited. Then he pounded on the door.

No answer.

Pro pulled out her cell and dialed the number.

"Front desk," came the big man's voice.

"Hello, sir, it's Detective Thompson. I didn't get your name."

"It's Luther. Luther Ardoin."

He stated his last name with a French pronunciation, and Pro found her knees grew weak.

"Ah well," Pro said, surprised she was short of breath. "Did Mister Mystique leave at some point?"

"No, detective. We saw him last night about 7:00. I suppose he could have gone out, but usually he lets us know."

Chu held his hand out, and Pro handed him the phone. He took it and spoke into it. "Can open his door with a spare key?"

"Is that necessary, detective?" Luther replied. "We try to respect our residents' privacy."

"I understand completely. However, if you could open his apartment just to make sure he's all right."

"That sounds reasonable. I'll be right up."

Chu handed the phone back to Pro.

Pro watched her partner carefully. "Are you going to claim exigent circumstances?"

Chu sighed. "I will in my report. I'm sorry, Pro, I just have a bad feeling."

"I understand. We are allowed warrantless entrance in, quote, emergency situations requiring swift action to prevent imminent danger to life or serious damage to property, end quote."

"No one can say you don't know the rules."

"Well, if he's just asleep, we'll have egg on our face."

"On the other hand, the LT can't be madder at us than he is right now," Chu fretted.

Pro gave her partner a knowing grin. "I'll try to remember you said that when I end up walking a beat for the next five years."

The elevator door opened and the tall, bare-headed Luther strode over.

Pro had to look down as she found her mind racing again with unbidden thoughts. What was happening to her? She hadn't had desires like this in at least a year.

"Detectives," Luther said. Chu nodded, and Pro just muttered, keeping her eyes on the floor.

Luther stepped up to the door, pressed the buzzer, and then pounded on it with loud raps. "Mister Mystique. It's Luther. We are concerned about you."

He pounded on the door a second time, and Pro couldn't help looking at his muscular rear end. She shook her head, surprised with herself that such a brief encounter had activated such feelings in her.

"Mister Mystique, I am coming in!" Luther hollered, and pulled a large ring of keys, and with a practiced hand, inserted one and unlocked the door.

"Mister Mystique?" Luther called out again. Only a dark room, and silence greeted them. "That's not good."

Chu nodded. "Mr. Ardoin, I think we have probable cause to go in."

"I agree, detective," Luther assented and stepped back from the door.

All business now, Chu and Pro pulled out their service weapons and pushed past Luther. They moved into the room, Chu going low and Pro high as they had practiced again and again. They both led with their weapons, eyes scanning left and right quickly. The room was fairly dark, as the curtains were all closed, but also stuffy, as if the air wasn't circulating.

Chu hit a light switch and the room blazed with illumination. The two detectives moved like a unit to the next doorway, and then past it.

Shouts of "Clear" came as the pair moved quickly from room to room, finally ending up in the bedroom.

On the bed lay a man, heavyset, with brown hair and a thin beard and mustache. There were ligature marks around his neck and a short yellow rope lay on his chest.

"Mike Mystique, I guess?" Chu said, holstering his weapon.

"That would be my thought. How long ago?" Pro gasped, coming down from the tension of entering the room with a drawn weapon.

"Not long," Chu said as he pressed his fingers to the carotid artery on the dead man's neck. "He's still warm and there is no rigor."

"There's a wallet on the bedside table," Pro pointed out. "Maybe it has his ID."

"I'll call it in," Chu said as Pro pulled out latex gloves and put them on.

Chu spoke quickly to the dispatcher and used the codes to let them know they needed forensics and the Medical Examiner at their address.

By now, Pro gloved up, and she picked up the wallet and gave a brief cry.

"What is it?" Chu asked. "Is that his ID?"

"No," Pro gasped and stared down at the leather billfold in her hands. "This is my father's wallet."

14. Multiplying Bottles

Hours passed, and the two detectives supervised the operation. Luther and his security guard partner, Jorge, were a very helpful asset when the other teams arrived and headed up to 12-C to view the former Mike Mystique. They could get them up the elevator with as little noise and fuss as a team of police entering a building could produce.

The room had quickly become a cavalcade of scientists and officers who examined every piece of Mister Mystique's belongings and life.

An officer arrived from the cyber division and asked to see the footage of the video surveillance in the lobby. Jorge escorted him to where they kept the recording machines so he could duplicate the footage from the previous night and this morning.

Pro and Chu moved to the hall as the investigators did their work. Pro had replaced the wallet where she had found it and watched a CSI technician photograph it and place it into an evidence bag before she left the room.

Though upset, Pro put on a strong face for her partner. "I guess I was wrong. My father is a murderer."

"You can't be sure of that, Pro."

"Then how did his wallet get here, Tom? We know locks don't stop him. He just walked right in and strangled Mystique."

"Pro, you're not thinking like a detective. You're better than this."

"What do you mean?"

"There was no struggle at the crime scene. You saw the room. Now if Max just snuck in and started strangling Mike, wouldn't he have put up a fight?"

"I don't know. Maybe Mike let him in. I mean, everyone knows Max in the magic biz. Maybe they were just sitting around talking and Max got the jump on him."

"Okay, let's say I buy that premise. Mystique's a big guy, got to be close to two hundred seventy-five. Your father is tall but lithe. How does he pick up Mystique and stick him on the bed?"

Pro considered this. "Yeah, you're right."

"I think the perp strangled Mystique in the bed. Notice how his shoes were off? Now, Max might have a lot of friends in the business, but why would he and Mike be talking in the bedroom?"

"Damn it," Pro said. "I didn't notice any of the details. Geez, I know better than that."

"It's like I said, Pro, you're too emotionally involved. You are a great homicide detective and a superb partner—"

"Really?" Pro brightened.

"But not on this case," Chu chided. "The LT gave us until Tuesday, but I'm going in first thing tomorrow and asking for this case to be reassigned. Your instincts are not working because of your personal involvement."

Pro's mouth became a hard line. "I've never asked to be reassigned from any case, Tom."

"I know. I admire your dogged determination and that you don't give up, believe me I do," Chu put his hand on her shoulder and gazed into her blue eyes. "But there is a reason detectives don't work on cases that are this close to home. As human beings, we just can't do it. Not even you."

"You're right," Pro said and clamped her teeth down to push back the tears that wanted to fall. "I'll do what you think is best, Tom."

"Okay. I think you should take tomorrow off. Unwind, relax, do something else. And then we can start Tuesday with a fresh case that's just simple, like a plain old jealous lover or something."

This got a grin from Pro. "Thanks for covering for me, partner."

Chu shrugged. "It's what we do."

Pro took the elevator down, her mind reeling. She felt like a total failure. She'd let her father play with her emotions, and because of it, three people were dead, and she should've stopped him after the first one.

What she wanted to do was ask that handsome guard out, get drunk, and show him a night they'd both never forget. But she knew that plan wasn't a good one, either. She just wanted a distraction from what she was feeling.

The doors opened to the lobby, and Pro noted that night had fallen. She saw Luther at the front desk as Jorge was explaining the situation to a distraught tenant, who was wearing only a housedress and slippers.

"Really, Mrs. Henley, you are perfectly safe."

The white-haired woman went on with an annoying whine. "They kill a man in this building and you say I'm safe? How did he get in? I want to know—"

With the noise going on, Pro went to the desk, and Luther looked up. He smiled his endearing smile. "I made sure your guy got copies of all the tapes, detective."

"I'm… uh… sure you did," Pro said, suddenly tongue-tied after her lusty thoughts in the elevator. "I just wanted to… uh… thank you for all you did. You were a great help."

"My dad was a beat cop. I have a lot of appreciation for cops."

"Really?" Pro said and found her hand went up to primp her hair. "My dad was, too — I mean, my stepdad. But he's the one who raised me."

"Seems like we got a lot in common, detective."

Pro stood in wonder. Honestly, the man had a voice like Barry White and Luther Vandross rolled into one.

Pro reached into her bag and extracted her card. "If… uh… anything comes up—" she blushed at the accidental double entendre. "I mean, if you hear anything, please call me."

He nodded. "I'll do that, detective."

"And… umm… if you're not married or anything —" she fumbled. "You're not married, are you?"

The smile grew broader and sexier. "No, I'm not, detective."

"Oh, good… I mean… as long as you're… I mean," Pro stopped herself and took a deep breath. "If you'd like to do something sometime or want to talk about anything other than work, that would be nice, too."

"That sounds real good, detective." He held out his hand and Pro gave it a quick shake, but he held onto it for a moment. "I'm very glad I met you, Detective Thompson."

He released her hand, and Pro smiled and headed past Mrs. Hanley, who was still complaining to Jorge.

The crisp spring air only bolstered the strange combination of emotions that were shooting through her nervous system. She headed for the subway to take the train up to her mother's apartment.

Fifteen minutes later, she phoned her mother as she returned to the sidewalk from the underground ride.

"Yes, dear?" came her mother's voice.

"First, is anyone there? I mean, besides you."

"No, and if Max was here, I'd be telling him to turn himself in. Where are you?"

"Heading up to your place. Can I come up and sleep in my old bed?"

"Of course, honey, anytime you want."

"Good! I'll bring wine, lots of wine."

"I imagine you'll have a story for me. I could make some dinner."

"I could use that, Momma. See you soon."

Pro walked into the nearby liquor store and looked at the wine. She got two and then decided three bottles would be the best choice. She sensed it was a good thing she had the next day off, because she planned to be completely hungover tomorrow. Maybe if she drank enough, she could forget about her father and all the crap he'd brought into her life, at least for one night.

As she walked out with her purse and attaché under one arm and the three bottles in a bag in the other, her cop senses bothered her.

She was being followed.

She had sensed it subliminally once she left the subway, but now she was sure of it. A person moving just out of view but matching her movements as she headed for her mother's place. And she was carrying too many things to make accessing her weapon easy.

"Pro," a voice hissed.

She turned, and in the shadows of a nearby doorway saw a tall, thin figure.

"Max?" she yelped.

"Sh! It's okay. I didn't want to scare you."

"Max, you gotta surrender," she said, fumbling with all the things she carried as she attempted to get to her service weapon. "You killed Mike Mystique!"

"I did not! I visited him this morning. He was fine."

"Well, now he's dead, and your wallet was on the nightstand."

"What? That's impossible. Did you get the box from Sam?"

"Sam Lovell gave me a box with your stuff, but your wallet wasn't in there! Have you been following me all day?"

"Pumpkin, calm down!"

"Don't you call me that!" Pro shrieked and fell to her knees. In a quick move, she let everything she carried fall to the ground and yanked out her service weapon to raise it in a two-handed grip. "You are under arrest!"

She stood and faced an empty doorway. She looked to her left and right, but no one was moving. Her phone beeped. She holstered her weapon and pulled out her phone. To her surprise, there was a text message from an unrecognized number which read:

Sorry, had to run.

The answers are in the

coded emails.

Good luck, pumpkin

She cursed quietly to herself as she picked up her dropped items. At least none of the bottles had broken, and she was grateful for that. But he had waited until items weighed her down to reveal himself so she would have to look away to get her weapon. That was when he did his vanishing act.

"I'm gonna catch you, Max," she yelled to the night sky. "And then you're gonna see some police brutality!"

Pro picked at the plate of Pasta Primavera her mother had made. The first bottle of wine was more than half-empty, and the glass in front of Elisha was full.

Pro's glass was empty.

"You should eat, honey," Elisha worried.

The room was still amass with flowers, but during the day, Elisha had trimmed back the flora and had organized it so at least they had a table to eat at.

"I can't believe he followed me," Pro muttered. She took the bottle and refilled her glass. She looked at her hands, which had finally stopped shaking. Struggling to get her weapon had rushed so much adrenaline through her system that it had taken time to calm down. "Where does he get off following me? Then texting me with a blocked-off number so I have no way to trace his phone?"

"He probably planned on that, honey. And as far as following you, I think he wants to help you find the real killer."

"Doesn't matter. As of tomorrow, Tom is taking us off the case. He's asking the LT to reassign us."

"That's a pity."

"It's a necessity. I can see that now," Pro said and gulped down a large mouthful of the wine. "I thought I could help because I knew the victims, and I thought I knew about magic. Turns out, it's better if the detective's father isn't the number-one suspect in multiple murders."

"Your father didn't kill anyone!" Elisha exclaimed.

"His wallet was on the nightstand!" Pro responded. "Okay, I had his credit cards and phone, but not the wallet. How do you explain that?"

"Well, obviously I can't, but that doesn't mean—"

"And escaping. He broke out of jail, and he planned to do it. That's even worse!" Pro polished off her glass and refilled it as Elisha took a tentative sip from her own.

"But what about what your father texted you, about going through those coded emails?"

"It is not my case anymore," Pro said. "That way, if he gets his ass shot, I won't feel like Oedipus."

"I believe Oedipus married his mother."

"Ew. Okay, I won't feel like… whoever the Greek lady was that killed her father."

"I don't think I know that one…"

"The point is, it's not my fault if he gets his ass shot," Pro said and emptied her wineglass in one long swallow.

"Honey, slow down. And I think you should eat a little something," Elisha fretted.

Pro looked at the empty bottle. "And I think it is time I opened another bottle."

She rose to her feet a little unsteadily and pulled out the second bottle from the bag. Elisha sighed, but Pro didn't turn around. Instead she bowed her head and her shoulders heaved.

"Honey, are you crying?"

"No," Pro blubbered, unmoving. "Could I please have a tissue?"

Elisha got up and grabbed a foil box of tissues and held them out for her daughter. Pro grabbed a handful and crushed the paper to her mouth to stifle another shuddering sob.

Elisha pulled her daughter close. "There, there now."

Pro raised her head, tears on her face. "Why'd he have to come now, of all times?"

"What do you mean, my sweet girl?"

"I finally really felt like a detective. The last couple of months with Tom, we've been closing cases and making a name for ourselves. He didn't look at me like I was the rookie he was stuck with anymore."

"I believe Tom thinks highly of you."

"And now this case, one friggin' disaster after another. With my father is in the middle of it all. And you slept with him."

"All right, that is enough," Elisha exploded, and stood up suddenly, which caused Pro to fall back in surprise.

Elisha stepped over to the table and grabbed her glass of wine. "If you wanna sit there and complain about your lot and my choice to spend a very nice evening with my ex-husband, I gotta tell you to put a sock in it."

"Momma?" Pro said.

"You haven't thought for one minute how hard this has been for me. You think I like the fact that your father is pulling this shit?"

"I... uh—" was all Pro could manage. She had not heard her mother lay down the law like this since she was a teenager.

"And look, maybe you have issues with your father. Lord knows I do. But he's your father, and you should be out there trying to prove that he didn't do it. If you ever loved him, you should at least be doing that."

"I... uh—" was all Pro said again.

"He gave you one simple task: to go through those emails. Did you do it? No! You are too busy having the Prophecy Adele Martin Thompson pity party."

Pro looked drunkenly at her mother. She believed it was the first time her mother ever used all of her names at one time.

Elisha went to her glass of wine and downed it.

"So," Elisha demanded as she put down the empty wineglass, "you gonna help or what?"

"All right," Pro grumbled. "But can I do it in the morning? I'm pretty worn out right now."

"Go to bed, and we'll sort through these emails then. I'll help you."

Pro got to her feet a bit clumsily, with the decision that maybe she'd had enough wine. "I've never seen you so mad before."

"That's because your father has pissed me off and so have you! Now get to bed. You have work to do tomorrow!"

15. Phantom Vanish

T he next morning, Pro dragged herself from the spare bedroom to the kitchen and turned on the machine that would prepare her coffee. Once the light changed color to announce the water was hot, she put a plastic cup of something called "House Blend" in the convenient chamber and started it to brew.

As the machine hissed and gurgled, it occurred to her that something was different. She peeked out into the dining room/living room area. Her mother had seriously reduced the number of blossoms from the previous evening.

The potted palm was in a corner, but the flowers were merely covering a few side tables, and the floors were unobstructed by any decorative plants. As she contemplated this, the front door opened and her mother came in.

"Where did all the forestry go?"

"The flowers? Oh, I merged what I liked and tossed the rest. I was just dumping a trash bag down the chute. Leave it to Max to go for a grand gesture that was not very practical."

"You liked it yesterday."

"I did. I liked the idea that Max wasn't playing games for once. Of course, with him breaking out of jail and following you, it appears I was wrong. I can only guess that he just can't seem to help it; he has to be the smartest person in the room."

Pro nodded and got her coffee, hoping the caffeine would help relieve her pounding headache. She took a sip and sighed.

Her mother crossed her arms. "Good thing I stopped you at the first bottle of wine. You were going for the second when I yelled at you."

"You haven't yelled like that in years," Pro said and shook her head. "Since this whole thing started, you've yelled at me and threatened to spank me."

This got a smile from her mother. "You had your bad times. After Max left, you acted out, and I thought I was going to have a real problem with you. But then I met Joe, and once he moved in, you straightened right out."

Pro took another sip. "He had a great technique. If I misbehaved, he would look at me with those puppy-dog eyes of his and say he was disappointed."

"Oh yes, I remember."

"That was enough for me. I did everything I could to make sure I didn't disappoint him."

Her mother moved past her into the kitchen and began to brew a cup of coffee for herself. "I worried about that sometimes."

"Why?"

"When you went to the police academy, I was always concerned that you did it just for Joe. I was afraid that it really wasn't your calling, but you were so focused on Joe being proud of you that you did it anyway.

Pro smiled. "You never said anything."

"I didn't want to influence your decision either way. I just worried, as mothers do."

"It was the right choice for me. I enjoy being a cop, and I especially like being a detective. I make a difference."

"And you always wanted to do that."

"Besides, somebody had already taken my first job choice, fairy princess."

Elisha chuckled. "That's right. I remember you walking around in that dress every day. We had to pull you out of it to wash it."

"So I guess cop is my second choice."

Elisha picked up her mug and sampled the brew. "Besides, fairy princesses don't get days off. Now, are we gonna go through those emails or what?"

"Might as well get started. I am officially off today, so now would be the time."

Pro reached into her attaché and extracted the box with Max's things and the returned printouts. She put it on the table and opened the lid.

"Are those Max's credit cards and his phone?" Elisha asked.

"Yes, he left them with Sam Lovell for safe keeping. That's why he didn't have a wallet or anything on him when he was arrested the second time."

"Because he knew he was going to escape and wanted them somewhere safe?"

"Best as I can tell," Pro surmised. "Now here, look through those. I have copies that are already translated."

Pro pulled out the copies she had made the previous morning. She separated them into two piles: ones she had converted and noted the actual message and ones she did not.

"I was doing it by date, so let's go through."

"Way ahead of you, honey," Elisha said and went from one pile to the other.

"Since I have only one set of codes, you check those, and I'll translate a new one."

Elisha nodded, looking from one paper to the other. "The ones Max left, he organized by date as well."

"That doesn't hurt," Pro said and pulled out the page where she had written the Houdini and alphanumeric codes.

The pair of them were going through the pages when Elisha noticed something odd. "Wait, if he arranged these in order of date, I have one that is out of place."

"What do you mean?"

"I mean, you translated the one before it, and the one dated after it, but not this one." Elisha handed the sheet of paper to Pro.

Pro looked at it. "That is odd. There should be a list of emails by subject line and dates with those papers."

"Here it is," Elisha said, as she extracted several stapled pages.

Pro grabbed the list she reprinted on Sunday and put the two pages side by side.

"Yeah, the list I printed up on Saturday has that email registered. But look at the printout from Sunday, it's gone! In fact, it states that no one emailed that account on that date at all."

Elisha frowned. "How is that possible?"

Pro shook the pages in her hands. "This case keeps getting stranger and stranger. Give me that email and let me see what it says."

Elisha handed the one page over, and Pro wrote numbers above the words on the page. She then checked the other code sheet and wrote out the message.

"What does it say?" her mother asked impatiently.

"I'm working on it," Pro snapped, her head down close to the page as she wrote away. She leaned back and inspected the page. "Looks like it says, 'Prototype is close. Need input. See at MS.'"

"Oh, now everything is clear." Elisha grimaced.

"I'm trying to think how it disappeared off the list."

"A trick of your father's?"

"I doubt it. He can do wonders with a deck of cards or a levitation, but not with computers. I can only imagine that someone hacked the police server, because we downloaded all the files from Al Floss's computer, including the emails."

"So someone with excellent computer skills, huh?"

"Yeah," Pro said absently, going over the last few days in her head. "Malcolm Shaut!"

"What?"

"He was a person who attempted to buy the plans. He writes software and made a lot of money at it." She snapped her fingers. "Plus, his initials are MS."

"How could he have a prototype?"

"He told Tom and me he has a workshop in his basement. Omigod! He could be btg@magic.us!"

"But why hack NYPD and erase just that one email?"

"If he erased all of them, we'd notice it right away. He just erased the one that had his initials!" Pro stood up. "I've got to get dressed. Malcolm Shaut could be our killer, and I bet that's where Max will be. That's what his text meant about me looking at the emails."

"Do you think so?" Elisha wondered.

Pro was on the move. "I'm jumping in the shower. Call Tom, let him know what we found."

In record time, Pro was clean, dressed, and on the move.

She grabbed a necessary second cup of coffee on her way to the subway. She headed downtown on the Number 1 local to get off at the 50th Street Station. Once above ground, she called Chu as she walked from Broadway toward Ninth Avenue.

"Chu," his voice came over the phone.

"It's Pro. Are you heading for Shaut's place?"

There was a heavy sigh over the phone. "I am walking there now. But I thought we had decided it would be best to withdraw from this case."

"Did you talk to the LT?"

"It's been a crazy morning. I haven't seen him yet."

"Good! Because I think we can close this case right now."

"I am only doing this because you're my partner," Chu protested.

"That's good enough for me," Pro said and hung up. She passed Ninth Avenue and strode up the block toward the brownstone. Her hand slipped into her jacket to touch her sidearm and reassure herself that it was there.

She reached the correct address and looked up the concrete stairs that rose before her. Like the rest of Shaut's building, they looked freshly painted and clean.

Pro stood waiting for her partner, who couldn't be very far away. Her eyes went to the wrought-iron fence that surrounded the front of the building and was about waist-high. Behind it, there was a door on street level. Pro decided it must be the basement, as one had to ascend the stairs to reach the first floor.

From where she stood, she noticed the door wasn't closed. You couldn't really tell from out front or on the street, but from her angle, it was noticeable.

She glanced down the block to see Chu as he approached. He was wearing a brown blazer with khaki pants. She waited until he drew near.

"Are we going up and ringing the bell?" asked Chu. "Or are we just going to stand outside and wait?"

Pro put her extended index finger to her lips and Chu quieted immediately. She pointed at the basement door, and Chu went up a couple of steps to view it. He returned and whispered, "You noticed the door was open?"

"He might have an intruder," Pro murmured. "One that has no problem with locks."

"Should we let Shaut know?" Chu asked quietly.

"Let's see if anyone is in there. We have probable cause to suspect there is a burglar."

"Or Shaut forgot to close the door."

They moved as a unit up to the iron fence. Pro lifted the latch soundlessly, and the pair moved through it. She carefully closed it, and they advanced to frame each side of the door. Chu was on the side that opened, so he cautiously grabbed the knob, gave it a very gentle pull, and it opened a crack.

Both detectives pulled their service weapons and pointed them up at the sky. Chu gave a nod, yanked the door open, and as he went low, Pro went high, and they both shouted "NYPD" as they burst into the room.

It was indeed a workshop with machines around the room. Pro recognized a lathe and table saw, and she also saw large work benches to set up projects.

Directly in front of the two officers were two large glass prisms on slowly rotating platforms. And Max Martin, aka Max Marvell, stood between them with his hands raised in surrender.

"Ah!" Max smiled. "You found the same clue I did!"

"Don't move!" Chu said, his weapon still pointed at the magician.

"Of course not!" Max replied. "This is what I was talking about! Shaut was stealing my trick, and he killed the others to stop them from getting it. You need to arrest him."

"Arrest him?" Chu said and glanced over at his partner with a look that suggested Max had lost his mind.

Pro lowered her weapon and returned it to her holster and then extracted her handcuffs from a pocket. "Look, Max, he got a couple of crystal thingamajigs on some platforms; that proves nothing. We'll press him about the murders, but right now, we need to arrest you!"

"Me?" Max said. "But this proves he's the killer. He was building Prism!"

"Max, put your hands behind your back," Pro said as she approached her father. "Once we have you locked up, we will talk to Shaut."

She pulled Max's hands behind him and fastened the cuffs.

"You don't understand," Max whined as the metal was slid around his wrists.

"Actually, we do, Mister Martin," Chu said as he holstered his weapon. "You are an escaped fugitive and a flight risk."

Pro moved back to Chu to speak in quiet tones. "One of us should stay here and monitor the place, to make sure Shaut doesn't go anywhere."

"You take Max to the precinct. He'll be more cooperative with you."

They both turned to face Max, who stood only a few feet away from them. He was in front of an antiquated cabinet about the size of an old-fashioned phone booth. There was a curtain in place of a door, and open so you could see inside. The interior had alternating stripes of purple and light red that went up vertically from the bottom of the box.

"So you don't believe he got the plans for Prism? Then I'll prove it." Max stepped on a nearby foot pedal.

The two oblong prisms started spinning.

"Max, that will not help," Pro yelled, but both she and Tom took a step back.

There was a strange "whirring" noise and a high-pitched screech pulsated through the room, which made Pro and Chu cover their ears.

With one simple gesture, Max threw the open handcuffs to Pro's feet and held his arms aloft…

And was gone.

The effect was so startling that both Pro and Chu, their hands still over their ears, blinked in astonishment.

Pro quickly traced the foot pedal cord Max stepped on. It went to a small box with a blinking light. She went around the rapidly rotating prisms and followed the wire to a metal box with lights. It looked like some kind of pre-made utility box one would use for a home electronics project.

Still, she located a small red toggle switch, and with a flick of her hand, turned the unit off. The blinking light went out, and the high-pitched whine ceased.

The spinning crystals began to slow, and Chu moved into the place Max had stood. "Where did he go?"

Suddenly, someone yanked the door forcibly, and there stood Malcolm Shaut. He was breathing hard, as he obviously had just ran out of the house, down the stairs, and to the door.

"What are you doing here?" he panted as sweat rolled down the side of his face.

16. Cabinet Escape

U niformed officers were at the brownstone and forensic investigators were conducting a thorough investigation.

Upstairs on the first floor, Pro and Chu sat across from Malcolm Shaut as he looked from detective to detective.

"So you are btg@magic.us," Pro accused.

"I have no idea what you are talking about!"

"We cracked your use of the Houdini code. Honestly, do you think we're stupid?"

Shaut looked desperately at Chu. "Has she lost her mind?"

"And then you hacked the NYPD servers and erased the message." Pro pulled a folded paper from her pocket and slapped it down onto the desk. "Here! Read it yourself!"

"I'm a software developer, not a hacker, and I've hacked no one!" Shaut carefully picked up the creased sheet and opened it. He looked at it for a moment, then tentatively put it down and glared at Pro. "I didn't write this or send it."

"Oh, I see," Pro demanded angrily. "So why did you neglect to let us know you had a working prototype of Prism?"

Chu cleared his throat. "It seems odd, Mister Shaut, that you were trying to get plans for the trick while you have a working version in your basement."

"Look, I'm telling you, I didn't write that email, and I don't even have an email account like that. As far as what I have in the basement, that was me tinkering away. Floss gave me a rough idea of the size of the prisms used in the effect and the spinning platforms, so I had those made. I also figured out the control box with my assistant. We hooked up the electronics to make the platforms rotate. But I couldn't get the trick to work."

"We just saw it work," Pro said while gesticulating wildly. "It made Max disappear!"

"All I can think is that he got it functioning somehow. You said you found him there. Do you have any idea how long he'd been there? I only came down because of the noises I heard. I recognized that high-pitched whine from the previous tests we had done."

"So where did Mister Martin go?" Chu demanded.

"I have no idea. From what I was told by Floss, it doesn't really make anyone disappear; it somehow bends light around a center point."

"What?" Chu said, as he stood up to lean across the desk. "How is that even possible?"

Shaut stood up as well and leaned on the desk so his face was inches from Chu's. "That's why I wanted to buy it."

"So I will repeat myself," Chu said, not moving an inch. "Where did Max go?"

Shaut backed down and returned to his seat. "If Floss was right, he didn't go anywhere. That's why Max used it as his last effect. He doesn't actually disappear; it just looks like he does. In his show, he would vanish, the lights would go out, and then the entire cast took their curtain call with Max in the center."

Pro got to her feet. "Then take us back to your basement and show us any other exits."

There aren't any other exits, just the one front door. When I had the renovations done, I even blocked off the stairs inside the building so that the only way in or out was through that door."

"Didn't stop Max," Chu noted.

"Believe me, I will have my assistant upgrade my security system to include that door from now on," Shaut said as he rose and followed Pro as she headed out of the building.

"And you're the only one who goes down there?" Pro asked over her shoulder.

"Only me and my assistant," Shaut said, as they stepped outside and walked down the concrete stairs.

"Where is Brent today?" Chu asked.

"It's one of his half days. He'll be here later to juggle phones if there is an emergency, so we can both get ready for the show tonight."

"That's right," Pro said. "A Night Of Wonder is in an off-Broadway theater every Monday night."

"For twenty-six years," Shaut pointed out proudly. "It is the longest running magic show in New York —maybe the world!"

They reached the sidewalk, and Shaut stopped. "Hey, you guys ought to come to the show tonight! It's usually a sell-out, but I am sure I can find some seats for a pair of New York's finest!"

"Mister Shaut, we really don't—" Chu began.

"We'd be delighted," Pro quickly put in. Chu looked at her with surprise, but she gave him a nod, and he made no objections.

"Great! I'll arrange it as soon as Brent gets here. Two tickets under the name of Chu, okay?"

"That will be fine," Pro said as they moved past the two uniformed officers, which were Bailey and Barker again.

Chu stopped and turned to Barker, who smiled. "CSI all done?"

"Yes, sir, everyone left, detective," she said, trying to be serious but smiling, anyway.

Pro noticed Chu gave her a wink.

They stepped into the workshop. The crystal prisms were stationery, and everything looked the same.

"All right, so where was he when he disappeared?" Shaut demanded, and went to the nearby control box and activated the power switch.

Chu stepped into the spot Max had achieved his vanishing act. "He was here, about two feet in front of this box." He indicated the cabinet with the purple and light-red stripes inside.

"Hmm. Well, let's give it a go," Shaut said and activated the machinery.

"Are you sure this is safe?" Pro exclaimed.

"I'm not sure of anything," Shaut said as the prisms spun.

"What should I do?" Chu questioned.

"Just stand there," Shaut said, and hit a button. There was the odd whirring noise again, and the tall crystals spun madly, but Chu was there and quite visible. The deafening whine forced Pro to cover her ears again, and after about thirty-seconds, Shaut hit another button and turned it off.

"Doesn't work now," Shaut said as the rotating platforms slowed down and the noise ceased.

Pro looked at the box Shaut held. "Where's the foot pedal? And the thing attached to it?"

"What?" Shaut said, and turned the box over in his hands. "There's no foot pedal, and no way to attach one."

Chu walked over. "We both saw Max use a foot pedal."

Pro nodded. "Yes, and when I hit that red power control, a cord from the foot switch ran to a small box about the size of a pack of gum." She pointed at a spot on the box where there was a perfectly round hole. "It was right there."

"So he brought something along to make it work," Shaut grumbled. "He must have been here earlier and figured out what was missing." He put the box down. "That crazy bastard."

"We still don't know where he went," Chu said.

"That I might help you with," Shaut said and moved past Chu to the large cabinet. "You said he was standing in front of this box, right?"

Chu crossed his arms. "Yes, so what?"

"I'll show you," Shaut said, as he stepped into the cabinet and drew the curtain closed along the front.

"He didn't go into the box or close the curtain," Chu complained.

"Well then," came Shaut's voice from the box. "Open the curtain and look!"

Chu walked up and yanked the curtain aside and gasped. The cabinet was empty.

Pro smiled and shook her head as she drew closer. "I didn't recognize it. That's a mirror cabinet."

"Right you are!" came the disembodied voice from inside the box. "Perhaps you will allow me to reappear?"

Pro stepped over and pulled the curtain closed. A moment later, Shaut slid the curtain aside and stepped onto the floor.

Chu, dumbfounded, walked over and stepped into the box, but everything appeared normal. "What just happened?"

"Some basic tricks in the magic lexicon," Pro said, then turned to Shaut. "May I show my partner how it works?"

"You know how to use it?" Shaut asked, an eyebrow raised.

Pro glanced into the empty box and nodded. "I think I can work the gimmick."

"Gimmick?" Chu said, still in the box, looking around. "I can barely fit in here!" He tapped the back wall. "Where did you go, out the back?"

"He went nowhere," Pro explained. "Here, step out and I'll show you."

Chu shrugged and stepped to the floor, and Pro got into the box.

"Okay impress me," Chu grunted.

"Let me just explain it," Pro said. "You see these vertical stripes? They catch your eye."

"I guess, but that doesn't explain where Mister Shaut or Max went."

"What you don't know is that there are two hinged mirrors on both side walls of this cabinet. They paint the backs of the mirrors with these stripes," Pro said. "There are also the same designs under the mirrors. This creates the illusion the box is empty."

"I still don't get it," Chu insisted.

"I'll show you," Pro said as she got into position. "When the curtain is closed, all I have to do is pull two cloth tabs on each side."

She pulled a small piece of cloth on the inside of the cabinet that Chu hadn't noticed. There was a shimmer of light as the right wall slid into the box to cover her. She then pulled the other tab and the left one moved. The two mirrors met in the middle and, once in place, they reflected the striped inner wall.

Pro was behind the reflective panes and unseen, yet the box looked the same as when it had been empty.

"Well, I'll be damned," Chu wondered and scratched his head.

"And to get out," Pro's muffled voice said from in the box, "you just push them back into place."

The walls of the box shimmered as the large mirrors slid back into their original positions, and Pro was back.

"I hope you know that both of you are now sworn to secrecy!" Shaut said. "I don't want you giving away one of magic's best tricks."

"That is impressive, but it isn't what happened," Chu asserted. "He didn't get anywhere near that box, and we would've seen him if he did."

"Not if the prisms actually bent the light around him," Pro said. "I think I get it now. The prisms refract the light in such a way that it creates a blank space. If the magician is standing directly in the correct position, it looks like he vanishes."

"But how did he get in the box, if that's where he went?" Chu said, still unsure of the premise.

"It created the blank space right in front of the box. All he had to do was step into it, pull the mirrors into place, and we'd never even see him. Think about it. We were looking at the foot pedal and control box to shut off the spinning prisms, which distracted us. In that moment, he stepped into the box and pulled the mirrors."

Chu frowned. "Okay, let's say I buy that. Where did he go after that? He's obviously not in the box now."

"He'd have to sneak out," Shaut suggested.

"No, we were here until the uniforms and the CSIs arrived," Chu said.

"The CSIs!" Pro announced and rushed to the door.

"Is she always this hyper?" Shaut asked.

"You have no idea," Chu sighed.

Bailey and Barker came into the room, led by Pro.

"Officers, I have a very important question for you. How many CSI investigators were on this scene?"

"Two," Bailey answered.

"No," Barker corrected, "it was three."

"I only saw two go in," Bailey said, knitting his brows.

"Detectives," Barker said a bit defensively, "I am sure I saw three leave. Remember, Bailey, the two headed for their vehicle, and about a minute later, the third guy came out."

"Right, that's right," Bailey brightened. "The one in the white coveralls."

"Yes, with the face mask and the hood on," Barker added.

"He gave us a thumbs up as he went out."

"By any chance," Pro interjected, "was he about six-two?"

Both officers nodded.

"Yeah, that sounds about right," Bailey said.

"Thank you, officers, you can return to your posts, please," Pro said and turned to Chu and Shaut. "I guess we now know how he got out of here."

"If that's correct, then he had a CSI coverall here," Chu said.

"Probably hidden in the box," Pro nodded. "He could have just changed in there."

Shaut looked at them both with concern. "Look, you guys gotta protect me. Max has killed two people—"

"Three," Chu said without a beat.

"Three?" Shaut bellowed. "Who?"

"We found Michael Mystique yesterday, Mister Shaut," Pro remarked.

"Strangled like the others," Chu put in.

"See! I'm in danger. He can pick any lock!" Shaut panicked.

"Calm down, Mister Shaut. We will leave the officers here to guard your house, and Detective Chu and I will escort you to your show tonight."

"Detective Thompson, may I speak with you?" Chu said.

"Excuse us, Mister Shaut," Pro said and stepped over with Chu to a corner of the workshop.

"I thought we agreed to ask for reassignment?" Chu whispered.

"We're going to be taken off of it tomorrow anyway," Pro told him quietly. "And who knows, if Max is really after Shaut, maybe we can catch him. Besides, you'll get to see a great magic show tonight."

"To be honest, I've had quite enough magic. So far, all it has done is give me a headache."

"You've only put up with it for a few days. I've dealt with it since I was a toddler."

"All right. But I'll need a couple of hours to clear my paperwork, and then I can go with you."

"I have the day off anyway. I'll babysit Shaut."

Chu nodded, and the pair returned to Malcolm Shaut.

"I will be escorting you today, sir," Pro explained. "My partner will join us when it is time to leave for the show."

"What is going on?" Brent Williams asked as he stepped in. "Why are those policemen at the door? I had to explain to them I work here."

"We had a break-in, Brent," Shaut said. "We need to get an alarm on this downstairs door!"

"Who could have broken in?" Brent stated, aghast.

"Max Marvell, that's who," Shaut declared. "That's why we need an alarm! That man is dangerous."

Brent turned to the detectives. "Did you catch him? Is that fiend off the streets?"

"Max Marvell is hardly a 'fiend,' Mister Williams," Pro objected.

"I believe anyone who kills people is a fiend!" Brent stated haughtily.

"The answer is no," Chu explained. "He got away."

"And he used Prism to vanish in front of us," Pro added.

"He used Prism?" Brent gasped. "Here?"

"Yes, it surprised Mister Shaut that it was functional at all," Pro went on, watching Brent intently. "He told us he couldn't even make the platforms rotate."

"I... uh... worked on it in my free time," Brent admitted.

"Did you?" Shaut said. "But you kept telling me that buying the plans was the only solution."

"I know how important it was to you. I thought if I could make it work, it would please you."

"You hear that!" Shaut boasted. "This is the kind of people I hire. He put in extra time on his own to make me happy."

"But how did Max get it to work?" Williams said as he walked to one of the oblong crystals and looked at it carefully.

"He attached a foot pedal and some kind of little box about the size of a pack of gum," Pro said.

Brent frowned. "It must have contained a computer chip and the software to run the machine. That was my problem, getting the prisms to spin at the right speed and in the right directions."

"How did he know what would work with what you built?" Chu asked.

Williams shrugged. "He must have snuck in here to see what I'd come up with." He turned to Pro and Chu, his eyes wide. "That means he's been here—more than once."

"I'm lucky he didn't murder me in my sleep!" Shaut blurted.

Brent Williams looked at the detectives angrily. "You must protect Mister Shaut."

"I intend to," Pro said. "I will be by his side for the rest of the day and will personally escort him to the theater."

"Just you?" Williams sneered.

"We will post officers Bailey and Barker here until we return from the show tonight."

"And after that?" Williams insisted.

"After that, we will see," Pro said. "There is an APB out on Max and they could pick him up at any minute."

"Hmph!" Williams grunted. "But not by you."

"What's that supposed to mean?" Pro growled.

"Nothing that isn't obvious," Williams said, chin held high. "You've had several opportunities to capture Marvell, and yet each time he slips through your fingers."

"So what?"

"The person helping him get away is none other than his own daughter, who is a detective at NYPD." Williams stepped closer. "I heard he got out of a holding cell at your precinct."

Pro's back straightened, and she seemed to become taller next to the man. Though they were both five-eleven, Pro seemed to grow and tower over him as her cheeks grew flushed.

"I would never help a prisoner escape," Pro hissed with vehemence.

"But you have to admit," Shaut said, and leaned against the table saw, "he always seems to escape when you're nearby."

Pro crossed her arms. "Are you suggesting—"

Shaut stood and raised his hands defensively. "It's just weird, that's all. You say you recognized the mirror cabinet. Why didn't you know what it was earlier, when you could've caught the guy?"

"He has a point, detective." Brent smirked.

"Detective Thompson is assigned to Mister Shaut as your protection," Chu said. "Officers Bailey and Barker will remain here to watch the residence." He stepped toward the door. "What time do you go to the theater, Mister Shaut?"

"6:00 PM," Shaut replied.

"Good. I will return then." Chu gave a nod to Pro, who was still actively working to control her temper, and went out the door.

"Why don't you head upstairs, Mister Shaut?" Williams announced. "I'll clean up and lock up down here."

"Good idea, Brent. I have some things to do in the office," Shaut replied and headed out the door, as Pro followed him outside. "Detective, would it be possible for you to get some coffee?"

Pro's jaw flexed as she fought to control herself. "Sir, I—"

There was a scream from inside the workshop. Without a pause, Pro pushed Shaut to the ground, leapt past him, and crouched at the door with her service weapon drawn out in a two-handed grip.

"What is it!" Pro demanded, seeing Brent Williams standing near one of the large pieces of equipment she thought was a lathe. She jumped to her feet and strode over, her weapon pointed at the ceiling.

On top of the machine was a letter-size piece of paper. Printed in bright-red letters was the word:

MURDERER

Pro looked to Williams, who turned to her wild-eyed. "This is the work of Max Marvell! How dare he accuse Mister Shaut of being a murderer! He's the killer!"

He grabbed the paper and tore it in two before Pro could say anything.

"Wait!" she finally said. "I don't get it. Forensics went through this room. Why didn't they find it?"

"It was under a cloth that covered the machine," Williams whined. "Hidden so that Mister Shaut would find it. Detective, you have to protect us!"

"I intend to, Mister Williams," Pro said, holstering her weapon. "Why don't you accompany us upstairs and lock this room for now?"

He nodded and made his way toward the door with Pro following. But she glanced back to take a last look at the ripped sign as it lay on the floor.

17. Mismade Lady

P ro spent the early afternoon in sheer boredom. She sat in the small waiting room between the offices of Malcolm Shaut and his assistant. Shaut made phone calls and clicked away at his computer keyboard, and Brent Williams who worked at his own computer and answered his own phone calls.

She sent Bailey for coffee instead of going herself, as she wanted to make Shaut happy and really needed another cup herself. She even asked Brent Williams if he wanted anything, but he passed.

"I make tea in the kitchenette next to my office," he explained. "I also make Mister Shaut his coffee, but in the afternoon he likes something special."

"So I've learned," Pro agreed. When Shaut had put in his order, it had been for a very fancy drink with a long name and an odd arrangement of ingredients.

For herself, she ordered plain black coffee.

Bailey had returned quickly as there was a Starbucks a few short blocks away, and had also bought coffee for himself and his partner.

Now, fueled with fresh caffeine, Pro pulled out her cell phone and tried to see if she could glean anything else from her father's message of the previous night:

Sorry, had to run.

The answers are in the

coded emails.

Good luck, pumpkin

She wished she had brought them with her so she could continue to translate them.

She still didn't have any answers. Someone erased the email she found from the server — who erased it? Was it a hacker or was someone in NYPD Cyber trying to ruin her case? And what secrets still lay in the emails she hadn't rendered into the genuine message?

And why were people continuing to be killed? Had the murderer gotten the plans from Al Floss? If so, why kill Tanner and Mystique? And what did Max have to do with it, and why was he continuing to pull his disappearing act? If he knew who did it, why couldn't he just tell Pro and let her and Tom do their jobs? Didn't he trust her?

Maybe her father truly didn't trust anyone. She had to admit she had issues with him, but since his arrival, he had not been acting like a rational person. The escape from the holding cell alone was enough to suggest that he was neither responsible nor thinking things through clearly. Sure, he escaped, and now he was the most sought-after fugitive in New York.

She shook her head and went to put her phone away when it rang and the name TOM CHU appeared on the screen.

"This is Pro. What's up, Tom?"

"Have you seen a television today?"

"No," Pro said and got to her feet. "What's wrong?"

"Ask Shaut to tune in Channel Four. They are about to show something you need to see."

Pro pressed the phone to her shoulder and walked into Malcolm Shaut's office. "Sir, how do you turn on the TV in the room I'm in?"

"What?" Shaut said and looked up. He rose from his desk and went into the waiting room where Pro had been sitting. He yanked open a hidden drawer on the coffee table, extracted a remote control, and pointed it at the screen, which came to life. "Is that what you need?"

"Yes, please, Channel Four."

Shaut hit a number on the remote, then handed it to Pro and returned to his office.

"Thank you," Pro told Shaut as he left. She then spoke into her phone. "Okay, I've got it."

"And we are both going to get it," Chu grunted.

The screen was tuned to the correct station, and a pair of clean-cut news anchors were sitting side by side at a large desk. The man, who had a smile that suggested expensive dentistry, turned to his cohost and smirked. "Rough day for the NYPD, Carole."

The blonde co-host, obviously Carole, grinned a practiced dimpled smile and replied, "You're right, Frank. Video footage given to Channel Four clearly shows that they have trouble keeping people in their cells."

"No, God, please no," Pro whimpered, as the image changed to the holding cell occupied by her father.

The News channel added enhancements that highlighted the unlocking of the cell, and arrows that showed Max's escape route.

The male host continued speaking. "Indeed, they do. Of course, it turns out they had arrested none other than the famed Las Vegas magician, Max Marvell. As you can see from the footage, he could pick the cell lock in mere seconds, and then walked right out disguised as an NYPD officer."

The camera went back to the artfully dimpled Carole, who was saying, "I think there are going to be some people in trouble at NYPD."

Frank appeared and glanced back at his shapely associate. "It is an embarrassing situation, as Max Marvell is over sixty-two years old and got out of the cell in less than sixty-two seconds. I guess this proves the old guy still has some skills, Carole."

The camera centered on Carole as she continued, "In other news tonight—"

Pro pressed the button to shut off the television, as she forced herself to stay calm. She walked through the apartment door and into the hall and put the phone to her ear. "You still there, Tom?"

"They haven't thrown me out of the building yet. But I expect the LT at any moment to do that very thing."

"I am so sorry," Pro fretted.

"This points to what you said about the NYPD servers being hacked. How else could anyone get that video?"

"It not only makes us look bad, it hurts the entire department," Pro lamented.

"Pro, look, I gotta tell you it is only going to get worse. Channel Four has been playing it for hours, and once this goes viral, someone is going to find out you're his daughter. Once they do that, they are probably going to suggest this was all a publicity stunt with you as an accomplice!"

Pro sighed heavily. "I'll fix it, Tom."

"How can you fix it?"

"Easy. Tomorrow, I'll go to the LT and resign," Pro said as she fought to hold back tears.

"Pro, that's not the answer! You're a good cop. You have the makings of an outstanding detective."

"I won't bring shame on my precinct or the NYPD. Don't talk me out of it. I've made my decision."

"But, Pro—"

"In the meantime," Pro said, taking a deep breath and straightening her back, "I am still a cop for one more day. I'd better get to work."

"Okay, Pro," Chu said, defeated. "See you at 6:00."

Pro shut down her phone and stood in the hall, trying to contain her emotions.

So this was how it ended.

Her father had come into town, and in four days she went from being a rising star to having to resign.

Because of him.

She took a deep breath and called her mother's cell phone.

"Hey, Pro, I was just talking about—"

"Mom, I have to resign." She felt like the entire weight of the world was on her heart.

"What?" Elisha gasped. "Why?"

"It was Max," Pro said, as she fought to keep control. "The video of his escape stunt was just on the news. It's going viral."

"It got a disease?"

"No, Mom, it's going all over the internet." She gave a bitter laugh as a tear rolled down her cheek. "He'll be more famous than he ever was. I guess that was what he was after. My career be damned."

"Honey, I don't think your father would want this to happen. You've worked so hard."

"Well, I am going to solve this case. Momma, can you bring those papers I left at your place to me? I hate to take you from work—"

"Honey, I'm the head of the design department. I can take off as much time as I want. Give me your address and I'll get them for you."

Pro reeled off Malcolm Shaut's address, and her mother said a few soothing words, but Pro was still too upset to really hear them.

She ended the phone call, checked to make sure the door to Mister Shaut's office was closed, and allowed the tears to fall.

A half hour later, a taxi pulled up in front of the building. Pro walked briskly down the stairs to meet her mother.

Elisha stepped out of the cab with the box of items. She took one look at her daughter and pulled out several tissues as the cab pulled away.

Pro took them gratefully and blew her nose. "I must look terrible."

"You look fine. Your eyes are red, but you're fine," Elisha said, and pulled her daughter into an embrace. At first Pro was hesitant, but then hugged her mother back.

Elisha pulled back and handed Pro the box. "I put both sets of papers in them. I also left Max's credit cards and driver's license and his phone that was in there."

"Thanks, Momma," Pro said. She actually felt better, and sensed her self-control was back in place.

"Believe me, when this is all done, your father is going to get a strong talking to from me."

"I never want to see him again," Pro seethed. "Except in a cell."

"You figure out this case, and maybe it will all make sense."

"None of it makes sense, Momma," Pro pointed out. "You have plans for this magic trick someone is trying to sell, then three murdered magicians, two who own stores and one that — I don't know what the heck he did."

"Unless they murdered him for another reason," Elisha suggested.

Pro stopped and looked at her mother, stunned. "Yeah, that could be. Momma, I gotta get back to work."

"I'm going to walk around on this lovely spring day. I'm way ahead on my current project, and I haven't had a day off in ages."

This made Pro smile. "Enjoy, Momma."

"I have faith in you, sweetie. If anyone can figure this out, it's you."

As her mother walked away, Pro went over to the basement door, where both Bailey and Barker were standing. They snapped to attention.

"You two all right, need a restroom or anything?"

They both relaxed. Bailey spoke, "We're fine, detective."

"Bailey if you're here alone, you have my cell number if you need to be relieved?"

"Yes, detective."

"Good, Barker, could you come with me, please?"

"Yes, detective."

They stepped out to the sidewalk, where Pro could talk in low tones. "Barker, Julie, I need you to do something for me."

"What do you need, detective?"

"Go to the precinct and talk to Tom. Ask him to give you copies of the Medical Examiner reports on the victims."

"You want the autopsies?"

"Whatever Tom has that you can print up and bring me, okay?"

"You got it, detective."

Pro smiled. "Thanks, Julie, and you can call me Pro, okay? After all, you are dating my partner."

Barker gave a smile and headed down the block toward the precinct. Pro walked up the steps, back into the building, and inside the offices of Malcolm Shaut.

Sitting in the small waiting room, Pro pulled out her first set of pages and went on with the translation. It wasn't enough to know what the messages said; she wanted to know the person who wrote them, to see if she could get some insights. The email sender "btg@magic" might just be the killer, but she could hardly glean much about him from the quick messages.

Each one was only a brief sentence or two, and they comprised arrangements to exchange money or pass the final plans once the sale was complete. She decided most of the arranged rendezvous took place at a nearby coffeehouse. There would be little chance of either person being spotted by interested parties as they planned their sale.

So what went wrong? The messages between Floss and btg@magic.us seemed remarkably businesslike and simple. Make the sale, get the money, each take their cut. What happened, so that Floss ended up dead?

Who had the motive to kill Floss or Tanner? Well, it could be one of the buyers. Michael Mystique was one, and he ended up dead. But Adrian Novack, aka Adrianna Gray, and Sam Lovell had both been interested, yet they were alive, as was Malcolm Shaut. Yet, she didn't see any of the trio as killers.

And who hacked the email list and downloaded the video from Max's escape? And for what purpose?

Was there someone not yet seen who was manipulating events and murdering people who got in his way?

She focused on the next email, just as Barker phoned her.

"Pro."

"I'm at the door, detective," Julie Barker said.

Pro got up and headed to the door. "Any luck?"

"I have the three preliminary reports."

She opened the front door and Barker handed the papers in.

"Any trouble?"

"No, Tom was a gem about it. He said something about you resigning? Is that true?"

"Sorry, Julie, that was something he said to his girlfriend, and I'd like you to keep it to yourself."

"He was very upset about it."

"That's tomorrow, Julie. For tonight, please monitor that workshop, and I promise I'll explain everything tomorrow before I leave."

Barker sighed. "Okay. But I just want to say that you should think it through. Not just for you, think about Tom. He really relies on you."

Pro nodded and quietly shut the door. She couldn't bring herself to talk about it, as she was afraid the tears would return. She had one last night as a kick-ass homicide detective and wouldn't let herself go all weak-kneed now.

Back in the waiting room, Pro looked over the reports, comparing the conclusions made by the autopsy. What she saw hit her like a ton of bricks. She peeked into the apartment to see Shaut still working away. She turned the lock on the door so it wouldn't completely close and shut it.

She went to the end of the hall and called Tom.

"Is everything all right, Pro?"

"Yeah. Except my blabbermouth partner tells his girlfriend I'm resigning."

"Sorry, Pro. She knew I was upset, and I had to tell someone."

"I don't think she'll spread it around. Did you look at the autopsy?"

"I glimpsed over it. Pretty straight forward. Death by strangulation, using a rope to garrote each victim."

"Yes, but the ME concluded a man with a dominant right hand strangled that Albert Floss. Meanwhile, an assailant with a dominant left hand choked the other two victims. Tom, we might be looking for two different killers!"

"Or someone ambidextrous who is trying to fool us."

"That's a stretch. And if he could use both hands, it's the stance, the way he uses the rope, that decides the pressure on the neck. That's what led to the ME's judgment about the perp."

"Is Max left-handed or right-handed?"

"Jeez, I don't know. I never thought about it."

"Well, I am about to leave and join you to escort Mister Shaut downtown."

"What time is it?" Pro said and glanced at her watch. "After 5:00? Wow, the day went by fast."

"I assume there has been no trouble there."

"None. Shaut and his assistant have spent the day glued to their screens."

"Well, I think it is a good idea for us to not be at the precinct when that video is all over every channel tonight."

"See you soon," Pro said and hung up. She was ready to go back in when the phone rang with UNKNOWN CALLER as the ID. She thought of letting it go to voicemail, but she was afraid it might be Max and answered it.

"Hello?"

"Hello, is this Detective Thompson?" a deep voice said in her ear. The tone and the beauty of the man's voice made her smile despite herself.

"Yes, it is," she replied, surprised that she felt like a schoolgirl.

"I hope I'm not catching you at a bad time. This is Luther Ardoin, the security officer you met the other day."

"I-I remember you well, Mister Ardoin."

"Oh good. Please call me Luther."

"Delighted to, and you can call me Pro."

"Well, from our brief meeting, I could tell you certainly were a pro at everything you do."

What was it about this guy? wondered Pro. *Just his voice makes me all gooey inside.*

"That's… um… very kind, Luther," Pro said, with the feeling that she was babbling like an idiot.

"I was wondering if I could see you sometime, when you're not busy."

Starting tomorrow, I'm free as a bird, with no job and no life, Pro thought.

"Sure," she said aloud. "When would be good for you?"

"I was thinking either Wednesday or Friday, if you aren't working," he said. Then he gave a deep chuckle that also almost made her sigh. "Or tonight."

"I am… uh… on duty. But wait, have you heard of A Night of Wonder?"

"Yeah, that magic show in that theater downtown. You like magic? I'm surprised. A lot of ladies don't."

"You might say I was exposed to it at an early age."

"That's great! I'm a big fan."

"I'll arrange for a ticket. The show is at 8:00. I have to tell you, I am on duty. My partner and I are protecting someone."

"That's fine. Maybe you can give me a minute or two."

"I'll do my best, but you know what it's like when you are on duty."

"Very much so, Pro. Well, then. Until tonight."

He ended the call, and Pro felt her heart flutter. She shook her head. It had been more than a year since any man affected her that way. Maybe it wouldn't lead to anything, but she could have fun while it lasted.

Feeling lighter, Pro when back into the apartment and closed the door. She returned to the waiting room to continue working on the emails written in the Houdini code.

18. French Drop

T wenty minutes later, there was a buzz on the outer door that resounded through the apartment. Pro walked out of the waiting room and opened the door to let Tom Chu in.

"Are they ready?" Chu asked.

"Neither of them have moved." Pro shrugged. "Perhaps the pair of us can get them going."

They headed for the door into Shaut's office. "Any luck with the emails?"

"I'm about three-quarters through and found another pair of initials that the sender referred to as a 'potential problem.'"

"Really? What are they?"

"The initials are TM."

"Hmm? Anyone we've contacted with those initials?"

Pro shook her head. "But the message was weird. I'll show it to you later."

They walked through the door and found Brent Williams in the waiting room, where he was pulling a pair of plastic garment bags and a large suitcase out of the closet.

"Ah, detectives! Are you ready to roll?"

Pro looked at Chu and said, "Mister Shaut can ride with us, if that helps."

"Actually, we both are going to the show. Mister Shaut is the emcee tonight, and I'm also doing a set."

"A what?" Chu asked, unfamiliar with the term.

"He's performing as well," Pro translated.

"Ah!" Chu acknowledged.

Brent went on, "Therefore, I will need to talk to the other entertainers and make sure the stage crew has everything they need. You cannot bother Mister Shaut with trifles!"

Pro bit back her desire to tell the brown-nosing weasel to shut up. "Okay, well, we should get going."

"Mister Shaut?" Chu said and stepped into his office.

"Hm?" Shaut responded. "Oh, you guys go on without me."

Chu crossed his arms. "Sir, that would defeat the purpose of us escorting you."

"Oh, yeah, I guess so," Shaut conceded and stood up at his desk. "Brent, you got my—"

"Your tux is right here, sir," Brent Williams gushed enthusiastically. "It is cleaned and pressed since your last appearance."

"Good thing." Shaut smirked. "We had a dove worker. His damn bird pooped all over me."

"Pro, is it all right if Mister Shaut rides up front with me?" Chu said.

"No problem," Pro replied. "Brent and I can sit behind the divider."

"Divider?" Williams repeated.

"Yeah, it's an unmarked, but it is a police car," Pro explained. "Sometimes we arrest people and they have to go behind the metal cage. That's where you and I can ride."

"Oh, I don't know," Williams whined. "I get claustrophobic."

"For Pete's sake, Brent," Shaut scolded. "It's only for twenty minutes. You'll be fine."

Shaut grabbed a small briefcase from the corner of the room, and soon all four people were out front on the street. Brent put the suitcase and garment bags in the trunk, and with only a moment's hesitation, got into the car through the back door Pro held open. Pro slid in beside him, and Chu and Shaut got in the front.

Chu pulled into traffic, drove to the end of the block, and headed south on Ninth Avenue.

As they drove Chu glanced over at Shaut. "Is that all you need for a stage show, Mister Shaut?"

"Yup!" Shaut boasted. "I'm a minimalist. I just need a few things—some sponge balls, a couple of tricks I selected — and I am good to go!"

"So, Brent, how long have you been with Mister Shaut?" Pro asked in the back seat, as the blond man looked about the car nervously.

"A couple of years," he answered and peered at the door near him. "There are no door handles back here."

"Yeah, the only way out is to have someone open it from the outside," Pro instructed. "That way, prisoners can't escape."

"I don't like it," Brent muttered.

"It's only for a short time. So how long—"

"Two years," Williams interrupted. "Mister Shaut has taught me a lot about the business."

"What is your interest?"

"I want to do my own show. Create effects like your father does."

Pro looked out the window. "You don't want to be like my father."

"But he's created illusions no one had ever seen before. He worked in Vegas for over twenty years. That's a record."

"I suppose," Pro remarked coldly.

"And then to get out of an NYPD cell the way he did—"

Pro's head snapped back to Williams. "How did you hear about that?"

"It was all on the news. I saw reports about it online."

Pro leaned back and stared at the roof of the car. "Oh, jeez."

"You gotta admit that was pretty cool," Williams said, his fear forgotten in his excitement. "That's one reason I enjoy working with Mister Shaut. I can tinker in his workshop, come up with ideas. I'm the one who built that mirror box."

Pro's head popped up. "You built it?"

"Yes, and it was tricky. I had to glue the hinges to the glass with a special adhesive that can only—"

Brent went on, but Pro had tuned him out. The video was all over the news sites online. Her time as a detective was definitely over. The brass would see it tonight, and tomorrow heads would roll.

Hers first.

But if she resigned, she could claim it was all her fault for not securing the prisoner correctly. That way, Jacobs, Palos, and her partner wouldn't lose their jobs. It would all be on her, and as she was the daughter of the prisoner, the brass would buy it.

"And that's why I am learning to draw scaled plans," Williams was saying.

"I'm sorry," Pro responded, pulled out of her reverie. "Did you say you know how to draw plans? As in the ones we are looking for?"

Williams reddened. "Nothing of the sort. I said I'm learning to draw them. If you're going to build illusions, you have to know how to get your ideas out of your head and onto paper."

He faced front, and they rode on in silence.

"Oh, I forgot something," Pro said. "Can you arrange a ticket for a guest of mine?"

"A guest?" Williams said haughtily, and pulled a paper from his jacket pocket. "Now you're bringing a guest."

Shaut spoke from the front seat. "Brent, don't be an ass. If the lady wants a guest, give it to her."

"Sir, I meant no disrespect to the detective," Williams demurred. "But we have a very full house tonight."

"Stick him in one of the house seats we keep open. What's his name, detective?"

"Luther Ardoin."

Williams sighed. "Very well, sir. But we have that writer from the New York Beacon tonight, and you know how good press keeps us going."

"It'll be fine," Shaut declared. "So, a friend of yours? Someone special?"

Pro's voice became businesslike. "He's a security guard who helped secure the scene at Mister Mystique's apartment. I wanted to... um... thank him."

"Yeah, sad to hear about Mike. He was a good guy," Shaut surmised. "Sam Lovell must be pretty upset. I'm surprised he's still going on tonight."

"Why, were they friends?" Chu asked.

"Last I knew, they were an item, bumping uglies as they say." Malcolm chortled. "Of course, that's what the rumors were."

"And Lovell is performing tonight?" Pro asked.

"Yes, and Adrianna Gray as well. It's gonna be a hell of a show." He pointed at a building as they approached. "And there is the theater right ahead!"

Chu pulled the car over directly in front of the theater and into a spot which bore a sign that read "No Parking Zone." Shaut got out of his side of the car with his briefcase and looked up at the lit marquee that read "A Night Of Wonder" in bold letters. Chu opened the back door and Pro and Williams stepped out, then he opened the trunk and Williams got the garment bags and suitcase.

"Tom, I'll stay with our witness," Pro stated. "You park the car."

Chu gave a nod and got back in the car and drove away.

"So, I'm a witness now?" Shaut chortled.

"Yes, sir, that is why we can offer police protection," Pro explained. "Shall we go inside?"

The trio moved around the corner from the front of the theater to a metal door that Williams banged on with the flat of his hand. There was a click, and the door came open. There stood a young woman with dark-brown hair, in jeans and a work shirt, with a headset around her neck.

They were at a side door, just in the front of the first row of audience seats, and the stage rose up to their left with a set of stairs.

"Good to see ya, boss," the woman said, and checked her watch. "Whoa, 6:30? Is it a holiday or sumptin'?"

"Relax, Selly. I get here early sometimes," Shaut boomed in his loud voice. "This is Detective Thompson. She's my police escort."

"An' a not too shabby one at that," the woman said with a smirk. "I'm Selena, but everyone calls me Selly. I'm the stage manager."

Pro reached out her hand. "Nice to meet you."

Selly gave her a firm shake. "Nice arms. You must hit the gym a lot."

"I try," Pro said modestly. "You run the show?"

"As best as I can." Selly turned back to Shaut. "Everything the same as usual? Do you need to change music or anything?"

"Same as always, Selly."

"Good. I like it when things are easy. So, you want the roll call?"

"I'll be the one for that, Selly," Williams said, getting between the diminutive crew member and his boss. "Mister Shaut, you should start getting ready."

He handed Shaut one of the garment bags, and Shaut draped it over the arm that held his briefcase.

"Of course, Brent. Thank you, Selly, and I brought checks."

"Make sure you sign 'em this week, okay? I didn't like to have to drag you down here two weeks ago when you forgot."

"Already done, Selly," Shaut went on dismissively. He walked up onto the stage with Pro right behind him as Selly and Brent conferred on the acts of the evening's performance.

Shaut and Pro walked toward a large curtain that had a lit-up box hanging down on wires from the curtain rod. It bore the emblazoned logo for "A Night of Wonder" in fanciful letters. They walked into the wings, down a flight of stairs, and into a door marked "Dressing Room One."

"One advantage of being the producer," Shaut bragged, "I get the closest dressing room."

"Nice," Pro said, trying to be upbeat. The room wasn't very large and had peeling paint on the ceiling. There were several makeup mirrors with lights around them, but half of the bulbs were out. Above the mirrors were a series of shelves going up fairly high. Stacked on the shelves were props, discarded wigs, and items leftover from what appeared to be the last hundred shows ever done in this theater.

Shaut hung the garment bag on a rickety standing rack and put his briefcase on the small ledge built into the wall below the mirrors. It was obviously to be used for makeup. Shaut opened his case and arranged the contents.

He sectioned the case off into little squares, each one containing a different prop or accessory. He had added a sheet of foam on the lid, which kept everything in place and protected the contents in transit.

Pro could see props reminiscent of her own childhood, things she saw Max carry in a small case he'd bring to events. Red balls of various sizes made of sponge, a plastic thumb, a crescent moon-shaped object with a pencil lead, small enough to fit under a thumbnail.

Shaut took things out one at a time, did some simple preparation, and then unzipped the garment bag and extracted his jacket. He placed objects in the pockets, and a wad of fake fifty-dollar bills into a clip that hung down the back of the suit..

"Mister Shaut, if you don't mind, I'm going to check the perimeter," Pro said.

"Hmm?" Shaut said, without looking up, as he focused on his tasks. "Very well, I'll be right here."

She stepped out into the hall and looked to her left, where she saw several doorways emblazoned with different numbers.

Next to the hall were stairs to the stage, and another set of stairs that went up to a second floor. She quickly climbed them and was on a small balcony that had a pair of bathrooms. There was also a hallway with closed doors but no lights on. She looked to see if any light came under the door, but they were all dark. She decided they were extra dressing rooms, if the theater had a show with a large cast.

She returned to the first floor, stepped into Dressing Room Two, and pulled out her papers from the attaché she had brought.

Going through the stack, she pulled out the translated message that had troubled her. It had been from Wednesday of last week, so only two days before the murder of Albert Floss. In pen she had written the number and the words above it. It read:

Deal is close

Trouble

Must keep one ahead

Of TM

It was something about the phrase that kindled something in her memory. Bad enough she had to crack that Houdini code and count out all the words, but now the message had another meaning that she was unsure of.

The door burst open and Sam Lovell came into the room, which made her rise to her feet. He carried a small suitcase and had a garment bag hanging on a strap from his shoulder. He looked up to see Pro as she stuffed the pages away.

"Oh! Sorry, luv, didn't know anyone would be 'ere," he said.

"Quite all right, Mister Lovell," Pro said as she gathered her papers. "By the way, my partner checked your alibi for Friday. Your sponsor vouched for you."

"Just like I said." He gave a lopsided grin that showed off his crooked teeth.

"By the way, I heard from… someone that you were very close with Mister Mystique."

The smile vanished. "From 'ooja 'ear that?"

Now it was Pro's turn to smile. "Around. I was just wondering how much truth there was to the rumors."

"Look, Michael was me friend, that's all. Anyone says anything else, it's all lies."

"I see." Pro weighed her words. "Do you know of any reason someone would want him dead?"

"Look, Mike 'ad a thing about money. 'E was right greedy. If 'e 'eard there was a score going down, 'e'd try to muscle in on it. If you ask me, that's what got 'im done in."

"Well, thank you, that's very helpful. I was just leaving," Pro said and slipped past the lanky magician to go out the door.

She continued down the dark hall and opened the door to Dressing Room Three. Before her was Adrian Novack, aka Adrianna Gray, in nothing but a bra and panties, trying to curl her hair with a large electric curling iron.

"Oh hey, detective, c'mon in," Adrian said with a high-spirited voice when Pro tried to back out. "But shut the door. I don't want the boys to see the goods if they ain't buying, ya know what I mean?"

Pro, not seeing a way to escape gracefully, stepped into the room and quietly closed the door. The third dressing room was remarkably similar to the previous two. Peeling paint, many shelves with discarded relics, and the under mirror ledge, Adrian had spread out equipment and also makeup.

"How are you, Miss Gray?" Pro attempted to sound cordial.

"Good. Hey, honey, I gotta apologize. I was pretty stewed when you guys showed up at my place yesterday."

Pro shrugged. "It could happen to anyone…"

"Yeah, well after you left, I realized you're Max's kid. I certainly wouldn't have talked about your old man the way I did if I had known," she said and looked at herself in the mirror as she completed another curl.

She grabbed a small electronic cigarette off the table and took a drag, which she held and then slowly released in a thin cloud of vapor. "Not that I said anything that wasn't true. But Max actually was always pretty nice to me, though not interested in a physical relationship." The older woman turned around with a huge smile. "Hey, think of that! If

Max had given me a tumble, I coulda been your stepmother!"

"No, thank you," Pro blurted. "I have had quite enough stepmothers, if you don't mind."

"Oh yeah, Max did like the ladies. I once told him he should just bang 'em and not marry each one. Oh, but I shouldn't talk like that in front of you. I never met your ma. Is she a nice lady?"

Pro stared at the floor. "To be honest, she's the best."

"That's good, that you like her and all." She took another drag as the device lit up with a blue light and she expelled another mouthful of fog that smelled like peppermint. She held up the electronic cigarette. "You gotta excuse me. I like to vape before a show. It's actually good for my throat and gives me a kick of nicotine."

"Well, I should get back to Mister Shaut."

"Wait, wait. I heard that you and your partner found Mike Mystique after you left my place. Is that right?"

"That's correct. We believe he was killed by the same man as Al Floss and Louie Tanner."

"Oh? Well that couldn't be your father."

"Why not?"

"'Cause he was hiding in my secret room until you guys were long gone," she said simply.

Pro turned toward the woman and closed the space between them to pull the curling iron from her hand and put it on the ledge. "Run that by me again."

"Max needed a place to crash, so I hid him in my secret room," she said with a giggle. "I'm a magician. I got one of those."

In one quick move, Pro grabbed the arm holding the electronic cigarette and twisted it behind Adrianna's back and slammed her face down on the ledge.

"Ow!" Adrianna whined. "Go easy. I got a show to do."

"You were aiding a fugitive?" Pro demanded. "Give me one good reason I shouldn't take you to lock-up right now and put your sculpted ass in a cell."

"I was just trying to tell you that your old man didn't kill Mike Mystique, that's all. Ease up. You're hurting me."

Pro let the woman go and took a step back. "Let me make it clear, girlie. After the curtain comes down, you are on your way to interrogation. I'd take you in now, but I gotta keep an eye on Mister Shaut."

"Max didn't kill anybody, don't you see?" Adrianna yelled at Pro. She then rubbed her arm and looked in the mirror. "Geez, now I gotta start over with my hair."

Unable to stand the self-absorbed performer any longer, Pro stepped back into the hall and slammed the door. She quickly texted her partner and told him to meet her backstage. She would need all the backup she could get.

At least she now knew where her father had hidden out once he checked out of the Waldorf and disappeared. Pro now had an inkling that Gray's drunken confession the previous day was staged for her benefit.

And the ME said it was two different killers, or at least the possibility of two. And they found Mystique in his bed. Did a woman tempt him and then kill him? But did the time line work? Was there enough time for Adrianna to kill Mystique and then be back at her apartment to be interviewed by the police? If the entire drunken act was fake, there could have been. Pro had assumed she'd been drinking for hours before she got there.

Then again, Shaut had hinted that Mystique was gay. Did that suggest a man was the one to tempt him into his bedroom? The ME report and forensics didn't say the body had been moved, but it wasn't outside the realm of possibility.

She had an overwhelming desire to burst back into the room and twist Miss Gray's arm until she told her everything. She took several deep breaths to calm down. Adrianna wasn't going anywhere.

Pro would make sure of it.

She continued to the last dressing room, which had three guys all dressed in suit jackets, two had ties. There were also three cases similar to Shaut's on their makeup ledge.

"Well, hello," a forty-something man with a receding hairline, pencil mustache, and a bit of a gut said as she entered. "I hope you're a groupie."

"No, I'm NYPD," she said and flashed her shield. "And you need better come-on lines. Who are you guys?"

A thin man in his twenties spoke up. "We're the close-up performers. We go on during intermission."

"Yes, I'm Tony Chiano," the third man said as he did a rather nice waterfall shuffle, the cards flowing effortlessly from one hand to the other in a beautiful flow.

"And how did you gentlemen get into the theatre?" she demanded, looking from man to man.

"Side door in the audience," Tony answered.

"Yeah, but if we're late," pencil mustache answered, "there's a door at the end of this hall."

"Thank you," Pro said. "Break a wand."

Pro heard Tony ask, "How did she know that expression?" as she went out.

She went to the end of the hall, and just as "pencil mustache" had described, there was a black painted door she hadn't seen until she drew near it. Checking the crash bar, she secured the door. She realized only someone inside could open the door.

She returned to Dressing Room One and peeked in. "Everything all right, Mister Shaut?"

Dressed in a formal shirt and black pants with suspenders, he glanced at the door. "Everything's fine. Did you see if the guys working intermission are here?"

"Yeah, they're all in Dressing Room Three," Pro answered. "You have magicians doing close-up during the intermission?"

"Yeah, it's what makes our show unique. Magic from beginning to end. We've become a New York institution." He then paused and looked at Pro for a moment, then blurted, "But who wants to live in an institution?" He then hooted at his own joke with a big, boisterous laugh. "Sorry," he said as he calmed down, "that's a joke I use in my show."

Pro nodded, now concerned Shaut would do sophomoric humor for the entire evening.

"You might as well go out front. No one can get in here without Selly knowing it," Shaut said, and pulled a bow tie from the pocket of his hanging tuxedo.

"We are talking about a man who can pick any lock, and there is a door at the end of the hall. Are you sure you're safe?"

"The door on this side of the building doesn't have a place to put a key — nothing to pick!" he replied. "The door we came in is the only door you use a key besides the theater front door, and we don't open those until we let in the audience."

"Couldn't Max sneak in with the audience?" Pro suggested.

Shaut chuckled. "That's sounds like something Max would do. But be careful. Your dad is a master of disguise. You might not recognize him."

"I see," Pro considered the suggestion. "By the way, after the show, I am arresting Miss Adrianna Gray, aka Adrian Novack. It turns out she was harboring Max."

"What?" Shaut bellowed. "Damn, must have used that room she has hidden behind the bookcase." He shook his head. "If it weren't too late, I'd throw her out of the show and let you arrest her right now."

"It tempted me, sir, but protecting you is my priority."

"That's the problem with that broad: her brains are in her tits."

Pro frowned. "Sir, I don't find that helpful — or appropriate."

"Sorry," he prattled. "Just sometimes, I don't know what she's thinking. You have every right to arrest her, but she is the first act closer. I would consider it a favor if you could wait until the end."

"I can't leave without you, sir."

"I want to tell you how much I appreciate you watching out for me, detective."

"All part of the job," Pro confirmed, and stepped out into the hall as she closed the door.

She leaned against the door for a minute. It might be worth losing her job if she could get away from these insane performers.

The early years of her life had been so chaotic, and all because her father was an entertainer. It was always about the show, the last show, the next show, the show in a week. She realized that the people her father associated with were just like the people in these dressing rooms now. Self-absorbed, loud, pushy; was it performers or just magicians?

Pro heard footsteps and relaxed as Tom Chu walked into the dressing room area.

"You okay, Pro?" he asked with lifted eyebrows.

"I am now that my partner is here," she said. "Shaut suggested Max might skulk in with the audience. I want to go watch, see if I spot him."

Chu frowned. "You really think he'll come here?"

"I don't know what he'll do, Tom. But after his visit to the workshop and the sign that said, 'Murderer,' I think he's fixated on Malcolm Shaut."

"I'll keep an eye back here if you want to go examine the crowd."

"Thanks, Tom," Pro said and took a step up, then turned. "Oh, and it turns out Miss Adrianna Gray was hiding Max in some secret room when we were there."

"What?"

"I told her we are bringing her in for questioning after the show. I wouldn't mind sticking her surgically perfected rump in a cell for a few hours."

Chu smiled. "I think that can be arranged."

19. The Hanged Man

P ro stood in the theater's lobby as they opened the doors at 7:30 to let in the audience for the 8:00 show.

She stood at the top of the stairs and watched the people walk in as the stage crew did double duty as ticket takers. She also saw a few people go to the small window of the box office to claim and pay for tickets.

She kept her eyes moving through the crowd, watchful for someone the height of her father. But a bare-headed black man caught her eye as he walked in.

Luther glanced at her and smiled.

Pro felt her knees go weak, annoyed that she felt like a schoolgirl again. She was in her late twenties, and developing a crush was not a way to create a lasting, adult relationship.

She knew that from her last romance.

She walked down the short flight of stairs, trying to control the goofy grin on her face. "Hello there. You made it."

"That I did." He beamed. "You look great for a lady still at work."

"Let me make sure they got you," she said, and the pair of them joined the line at the box office. Pro still watched the people as they entered and made their way up the stairs into the theater.

Luther was about six-two, and with Pro being five-eleven, he bent only slightly and whispered in her ear, "Who are you looking for?"

"Is it that obvious?" she answered, eyes still on the crowd.

"To me it is," Luther murmured. "And don't worry, I know you're on duty."

"I promise I'll sit with you during the show."

"That's all I need," he smiled. "But if you can give me a rough idea of who you're looking for…"

"Fine," Pro said. "White, male, about six-two, tall, thin, probably wearing a disguise…"

"You mean like him?" Luther said and gave a nod of his head toward the stairs.

Pro had only glanced away to talk to Luther, but turned to see a tall figure with a hat, heavy glasses, an enormous nose, and a long beard.

"Gotta go," Pro said and pushed away from Luther and into the crowd.

The tall man had just given his ticket to one woman from the stage crew, who tore it in two and gave him back one half.

"Ticket?" the crew member asked Pro.

Pro stopped and flashed her billfold and spoke in low tones. "I'm part of the team protecting Mister Shaut. I gotta see the man who just went in—"

That said, she pushed past the befuddled usher and headed down the aisle. She noticed that on the stage; they had closed an outer curtain, which hid the logo in the light box from prying eyes as they readied the show.

But she fixated on the man. She looked him over up and down. Yes, the body type was correct. The man was Max's height and build. She couldn't believe her father would try such an old trick as a hat, beard, and a fake nose.

The man sat right in the aisle, and Pro went down on one knee next to him. She grabbed his beard and gave it a tug. "You gotta lotta nerve showing up here!"

"Ow!" the man said as he turned to face Pro. With a start, Pro let go of the beard that was still quite attached to its owner. The man's brown eyes looked her over in shock. "Do I know you, miss?"

This close, Pro could see that the beard was actually quite real, as was the large nose.

"Geez, I'm sorry," Pro said and got to her feet, embarrassed. "I mistook you for someone else."

He rubbed his whiskers. "It's nice a lady like you mistook me, but please be gentle next time."

"Sorry," Pro murmured and turned away. People were coming down the aisle to get to their seats, and she perceived what a salmon going upstream must experience as she attempted to return to the lobby.

She finally got out to see Luther step away from the box office, his ticket aloft. He approached her in two quick steps. "Was that your suspect?"

"False alarm. I pulled the beard of a guy I didn't know."

Luther smiled. "Why, Detective Thompson, I didn't know you were so forward."

Pro grinned despite herself and relaxed a little. "Oh, you don't know how forward I can be."

"I can't wait to find out," he approved. "I also asked for your ticket and you were correct. You're right next to me." He handed her the small cardboard card.

"Let me text my partner, and I'll join you right before the show starts."

"If you need help to subdue anyone, I have experience," Luther assured her.

She looked at his powerful arms and wide chest. "Oh, I have no doubt of that. Thanks, Luther."

"Anytime, Pro," he said and headed up into the theater.

She stepped outside and watched for any stragglers. She pulled out her phone and instead of a text, hit the button to phone her partner.

"Chu."

"It's Pro. Anything amiss?"

"Not here. I assume you checked backstage when you arrived?"

"Not much to see. Just the dressing rooms and the bathrooms on the second floor."

"Aren't there more dressing rooms up there?"

"Yes, but the lights were out. I figured no one was there."

"Okay, good to know."

"I'll keep a lookout here. I have that security guard, Luther, out here as backup."

"From the size of him, I think you're in safe hands. Seems like you two hit it off."

"So far. Been a long time since I dated, so I hope I still can read the signs."

"From the way he looks at you every time you're near, I wouldn't worry."

"What?"

"The entire time we were at Mystique's place, he was staring at you like a love-struck puppy."

"Thanks for that. Later, partner," Pro said as she hung up the phone. So Luther was mooning over her all the while. She was looking at him like he was the last lollipop on earth. Not a bad way to start a relationship.

Not a bad way at all.

She went inside the lobby, up the stairs, and took one last look around the theater, just as the lights dimmed. She quickly sat in the aisle seat next to Luther.

"I figured you wanted to be on the aisle," he murmured. It amazed Pro that even talking quietly he could sound so damn sexy.

"Yeah, thanks," Pro whispered.

Music began playing, an upbeat version of That Old Black Magic. A voice announced over the sound system. "Welcome to A Night of Wonder, and here is your host for this evening, Malcolm Shaut!"

The music shifted into a triumphant blaring of horns, and Shaut came through the closed curtain, resplendent in his tuxedo. Pro had to admit, he was much more impressive on stage than he was in real life.

"Good evening, and welcome to the show. I am happy to announce that as of this week, A Night of Wonder has broken the record for the longest running magic show in New York City!"

This received applause from the audience, and Shaut waited until it subsided.

"The record we broke was set by us at our last show," he said, which got groans from the crowd. "But all kidding aside, we have been running continuously in New York City for twenty-five years."

Another round of applause filled the room.

"I was fifteen when I started this show," Shaut kidded. "But seriously, we have some of the best magical talent from around the world, and I want to introduce you to our first act. Opening for us tonight is an act that always delivers. How about a hand for Brent the Great!"

The curtain opened, and Shaut stepped to the wings. There was a small table held up by a black metal stand center stage, which bore a three-tiered candelabrum. Music played, as Brent came out in a red velvet suit jacket, red tie with formal pants, and a wing-tip collar shirt. The crowd applauded as Brent acknowledged them.

Pro frowned for a minute. Where had he been backstage?

As music played, Brent pulled a candle from the holder. With a gesture, it seemed to melt and become a white silk handkerchief, which Brent put into his front jacket pocket.

He picked up the second candle pulled, the silk from his pocket to cover it, and it vanished. When he opened the handkerchief, a series of folded silks bloomed in the center of the white silk. More and more unfolded, until he held an impossible amount of different colored silks in his hand. Finally, as the last silk unwound, a small rubber ball was in the center.

He picked up the ball and set the silks on top of his table. He bounced it once, twice, and then threw it into the air, and it was gone. The audience applauded. Brent took the last candle and seemed to press down on the top of it. It shrank until all he held in his hand was the small, white rubber ball he had vanished moments earlier.

"This guy's pretty good," Luther whispered to Pro.

She nodded. Even though Brent had talked about doing his own act, she didn't expect his skills and routine to be so strong.

He took the small ball and bounced it, and all at once there were two. With the flip of his hand, there were three. He reached up and pulled a fourth ball out of the air. When he turned back to the audience, he had white rubber balls between the fingers of both hands, eight in total. The music stopped as he put the balls away behind his table.

"Good evening, ladies and gentlemen," Brent said in a powerful voice, so unlike the whiny one he used most of the time. "I want to share with you an effect of my creation that I have been working on for a long time. I will need someone willing to select a card."

A man raised his hand in the front row, and Brent asked him up on stage. He quickly had the man select a card and sign it with a permanent marker that appeared at Brent's fingertips.

Brent had the man return it to the deck, and after a series of clever shuffles, handed the volunteer cards and asked him to locate his selection. As the man searched the deck, Brent pulled out a clear plastic bag with slips of paper in it.

"It's not here," the volunteer explained, and Brent nodded in agreement.

"How surprising! Now, in this bag, I have all the numbers of the audience seats here tonight — literally hundreds." He opened the bag and let the man look and pull several out, and he noted they were all different. The man put the slips back in the clear bag, and Brent shook it up to mix the papers.

"Focus your mind, and reach in and select only one," Brent said. The volunteer reached in and held one slip aloft. "Read it!"

"Seat C10," the man said.

"The person in C10, please stand," Brent said as a woman stood up shyly. "Would you reach under your seat and see if anything is there?"

The woman folded up her seat and retrieved a white envelope from the bottom.

"Would you bring it to me, please?" Brent coaxed.

She brought it to the stage, where Brent took it, thanked her, and asked her to return to her seat. Brent ripped an end completely off and asked this volunteer to hold out his hands. He hit the envelope, and a card fell into the audience member's open palm. The assistant looked at it and smiled, then held the signed card up for all to see as the audience went wild.

"Thank you. You may keep that as a souvenir," Brent said as the man returned to his seat. "I have one more effect I want to share with you—"

There was a pop like a minor explosion, and Pro found her hand went to her service weapon. One light in the illuminated sign hanging from the backdrop must have blown as the remaining lights flickered. She relaxed and took her hand out of her jacket.

Brent looked back at the crowd. "Nothing important, folks, just a—"

He stopped as the audience was "oohing" and "aahing." He turned back to the sign as a line appeared over the logo in what looked like fresh blood. Then, suddenly, the lines linked to form a word:

MURDERER

The blood dripped onto the floor as it flowed out of the sign.

Brent went as pale as a sheet. He looked at the audience and then walked off-stage. The curtain closed quickly, and the lights shifted.

Shaut pushed his way through the front curtain. "Hey, hey, sorry, folks, but one trick went off early. That was an effect for later in the show, and we'll have to cut it now."

He looked over the crowd with a stuck-on smile, and Pro couldn't help the feeling that this explanation was a lie. She looked around the audience to see if she could find Max once again.

"He ain't telling the truth, is he?" Luther murmured to Pro.

"That's what my instincts tell me," she answered as she continued to observe the room.

Shaut performed a trick directly in front of the curtain. He had the audience raise their hands up and selected a man in the third row. The man came up on stage and Shaut did a trick with two brightly colored balls made of sponge. The ball disappeared from his own hand and appeared in the volunteer's grip.

When the subject went to return to his seat, Shaut insisted he wanted to give the man a present. He then offered the man a watch, and the volunteer looked at his wrist to find that the watch was his own.

The man smiled and shook his head in amazement as he sat to applause from the impressed crowd. Shaut ducked his head behind the curtain, then returned out front with a relaxed grin.

"It appears the show will go on! Our next act is the first lady of sorcery, Adrianna Gray!" He stepped toward the wings.

The curtains opened to reveal a sequined covered table and an old-fashioned set of stocks that would hold someone in place.

Adrianna hit the stage in a sparkling gown, and Pro sat up to take notice. She decided the illusionist must have slipped on a set of undergarments that gripped everything and pushed everything else up.

Her chest was so accentuated, it surprised Pro she didn't fall face forward onto the stage.

As the music played, Adrianna took out three large silver rings from a bag that lay on top of the sequined table. The music shifted to a slow, hypnotic theme as she held up the rings and showed them one at a time. She moved forward to the front of the stage and spun one ring at the tips of her fingers, and with a tiny ting, it joined to one of the other rings

She showed the linked pair, and then turned and brought the first ring up the arm to her shoulder. With a smile to the audience, she let it slide back down her arm and it re-linked with the ring in her hand.

As the routine went on, slowly and with an unexpected deftness, she linked and unlinked the rings in several amazing ways, finally forming a chain of all three. As the music moved to its climax, she held the rings up with her hands, covering the places where the metal met. With a flick of her wrists, two rings slid individually down her arms, leaving a single ring between her fingers. It was a stunning finish to a strong routine, and the audience applauded loudly.

She bowed and then moved to the stocks. "It is often that a magician saws a lady in half. I think this is unfair, and I would ask a brave man to help me by allowing me equal time in sawing a man."

A large gentleman raised his hand, and Adrianna called him up to the stage. The man towered over Adrianna, despite her heels. She had the man kneel, to which she quipped, "One of my favorite positions to have a man." She then placed him in the stocks by removing the top part of the wooden frame.

With the volunteer secured, she picked up a newspaper that bore the headline, "MAGICIAN GOOFS, CUTS OFF MAN'S HEAD." After showing it to the audience, she placed in on the floor where the big man could read it.

"Now we've had enough blood on stage tonight, so try to keep yours in your body, all right, sir?" she quipped.

She then pulled out an electric jig saw with a scary looking twelve-inch blade. She slammed a battery pack into the back of it and pressed the trigger a few times so that it growled ominously.

Then she inserted the blade in a track at the top of the stock and started it up continuously. It made loud grinding sounds as she pushed it across. It traveled over the man's neck and out the other side, where the audience could see the twelve-inch blade still attached.

A quick unlocking of the wooden enclosure, and the man was on his feet, taking a bow with Adrianna. As he left the stage, Adrianna joked, "Don't look up at any tall buildings too quickly. We want nothing to come loose."

For a finalé, Adrianna pulled out a clear bowl of water, a Chinese fan, and some tissue paper. Ripping the tissue to pieces, she put them in the water, then held them aloft, dripping wet. She squeezed the water from the paper as the music built to a crescendo. She opened the fan, and as she waved it, dry confetti filled the air like a snowstorm.

She moved to the center to take a bow as the curtain closed, and the house lights came up to signify that it was intermission.

"She was fantastic," Luther gushed.

Pro nodded her head. "I have to say she was. I am really surprised. Every time I talked to her, she seemed so scattered. I didn't think she would be so good." She looked over at Luther. "Wow, it's been so long since I did this."

"Did what?"

"Just go to a show. I mean, I'm on duty this time, but even so. I guess I've focused on work too much."

"Well, Detective Thompson, if you give this man a chance, I would like to change that."

Pro looked at him wryly. "Be careful what you offer, Mister Ardoin. You might turn a girl's head."

"I'm not worried about girls. Only the woman I'm talking to."

"Do you always say the perfect thing?"

"Working on it."

Pro stood up. "I have to keep moving, studying the crowd. Someone set up that blood thing that happened with Brent."

"Bit of a shock for Brent the Great," said Luther.

"What did you call him?"

"Brent the Great. That's how the emcee introduced him."

Pro stared into space.

"You okay, Pro?" Luther puzzled.

"Brent the Great!" Pro said absently. "BTG! He's btg@magic.us! I have to get backstage."

"Need help?"

Pro looked at the guard. "Could you go out front. If Brent makes a break for it, can you stop him?"

"I'm on it," he said and headed up the aisle.

Pro headed the opposite direction toward the stage. She passed by the tall man with the beard and glanced up into his blue eyes as she pushed past him.

A performer, Tony was doing a card routine in the first row. "A little close-up magic, folks! Going on right here, the magic never stops…"

She ran past him, up the stairs and through the front curtain. For a moment, she stopped as the lights were low, and it took her a moment for her eyes to adjust.

"Tom!" she hollered as she moved backstage and into the dressing room.

"Yes, Pro," Tom said, as he rose from the steps where he'd been sitting.

"Where's Brent?"

"I don't know. I was backstage during the show with Mister Shaut."

"He's btg@magic.us!"

"What? How do you know that?"

"He's Brent the Great! Is Shaut here?"

Chu pointed at Dressing Room One, and Pro pushed through the door to see Shaut in front of one of the makeup mirrors, loading his pockets from his case.

"Where's Brent?" Pro demanded.

"Brent? He was pretty freaked out by that sign leaking blood, and I'm still trying to figure it out—"

"I need to know what dressing room he's in!"

Her adamance surprised Shaut. "He's not on this floor. He likes to change upstairs."

"Up there with no lights on? Whose idea was that?" Pro said, as she vaulted out the door and bounded up the stairs, taking two at a time, her hand going to her weapon. Chu was right behind her.

She reached the top of the stairs and went down the dark hallway and kicked open the first door. The room was dark and she could see nothing. Her weapon came out in a two-handed grip as she hit the switch near the door.

Lights blazed on in the empty dressing room. There was no outfit hanging on the rack, no props or makeup on the shelf.

She moved into the hall and yelled, "Brent Williams! Come out with your hands up!"

She reached the next dressing room, and Chu kicked the door open in one move. He hit the lights on as she swept the room with her weapon, going high as he went low.

Someone had recently occupied this one. There was a makeup kit, and a small bottle of amber liquid sat on the shelf. There was also a garment bag hanging on the rack.

But no person was in it.

They dived back into the hall and to the final dressing room, which she reached first and put her shoulder to the door to open it. She reached for the light switch, hit it, and raised her weapon to sweep the room. The lights flashed on.

There was a garment bag on the rack, a small zippered bag on the shelf, and an open suitcase in the corner.

Hanging from an overhead pipe with a rope around his neck was Brent Williams. He had fashioned a hangman's noose, and a kicked-over chair lay on the floor.

On the mirror, scrawled with the marker he'd used in his act, were the words:

I DID IT

20. Quick Change

- -

P ro ran back to the stage, pushed her way through the curtain, held her shield aloft, and yelled, "Police! Everyone, return to your seats!" She repeated this several times as close-up magicians stopped in shock and shoved their props back into their pockets to head back to the stage.

Backstage, Chu phoned for backup, and Pro quickly texted Luther to announce to the audience members to return to their seats. She could hear his powerful voice like a foghorn cut in the lobby over the chatter of the crowd.

Pro slipped behind the curtain just as Shaut came over to her. "You can't do this! We have a show to do!"

"I'm canceling the show, Mister Shaut," Pro commanded. "I need you and the other performers to go out into the audience."

"We will not—"

Pro lowered her voice and moved close to Shaut. "Mister Shaut, your assistant hanged himself in his dressing room."

"What?"

Chu came over to be part of the conversation. "We need you to bring everyone out from backstage and help control the situation until backup arrives."

They could already hear sirens in the distance.

"I guess... I... but, Brent..."

"We will need to bring in a forensic team and a medical team through that back door, so one of us has to stay here to let them in."

Shaut nodded, and Chu and he went backstage to collect the performers. Pro knew her partner would make sure they touched nothing or put anything away.

She walked through the curtain, and several people stood. One man shouted, "You can't keep us here!"

She held her shield up again. "Yes, I can! This theater is now a crime scene and you are all witnesses."

A murmur went through the crowd.

"Ladies and gentlemen, we need you to cooperate with us," Pro loudly pleaded. "All we will probably need is your name and contact information. We should be able to let most of you go soon. But until we've secured the building, we must ask you to follow instructions from myself or other officers, as well as Mister Ardoin."

Luther raised his hand as he walked back into the room.

Pro looked over the crowd one final time. "Thank you."

The three close-up magicians were already in the audience and moved to sit in the back row. The other performers filed out through the curtains one by one: Sam Lovell, followed by Adrianna Gray and Malcolm Shaut.

Luther was helping people to their seats and came down the aisle to Pro. "I should sit?"

"Please, Luther. Thanks for your help. I'm sorry I —"

"You're on duty, I know that. I'm just glad I got to sit next to you." He gave a nod and a quick squeeze to her arm before returning to his seat.

Red and blue lights flashed in the glass doors out front as two police vehicles pulled up. Four uniformed officers stepped into the theater, one older white male, two Hispanics, and an African-American woman.

Pro held up her shield as the silver-haired officer with stripes on his sleeve strode over to her.

"Sergeant Carson, Sixth Precinct," he said simply.

"Detective Thompson, Midtown North Homicide."

"You're a long way from home," he observed.

"Protecting a wit," Pro spoke quietly. "Looks like a suicide, but we're working a series of murders in our neck of the woods. The suicide might be the killer."

"Whaddaya need, detective?"

"If you could secure the site. We'll need someone to get people's contact info, and we need to know if they saw anything unusual."

"Is forensics on its way?"

"We've called them, and the ME. Sorry to cause this mess on your beat, sergeant."

"No problem, detective. I will have to call it in to our homicide division as well."

"Whatever you need, sergeant. We're guests here."

"I'll call for reinforcements."

"We also need someone to be at the back door." Pro pointed at the curtain to show where it was. "It's the easiest way in or out. I'll show you if you like."

"Just a second," Carson said and looked back at one of the other men. "Hey, Quantos!"

One of the Hispanic men joined Pro and Carson, and the three of them went up the stairs and through the curtain. They moved to the back hallway, and finally reached the door. Pro hit the crash bar and the door opened onto a Greenwich Village side street.

"Can you keep an eye here, Juan?" Carson asked. "We'll send the ME and forensics this way. Where's the DB?"

"Second floor dressing room. I'll show you," Pro said.

Pro and Carson walked up the stairs and she took him down the dark hallway and into the third dressing room, where Brent still hung suspended.

Carson read the writing on the mirror aloud. "I did it?"

"Yes, while he was on stage, a sign had bloody letters that said, 'Murderer.' I believe he may have been responsible for killing three people."

"Couldn't take the guilt, huh?"

"Might be. Then again, we've gotten some strange forensics from the other murders. I want to know if he did this to himself or someone did it to him."

"You'll need the ME for that. I've got to bring in more backup. You got like two hundred people down there."

"Thanks, Carson," Pro said as they stepped into the hall. "I'll be right down."

Carson nodded and headed down the stairs.

Pro went into the next dressing room. She walked over to the small bag about the size of a shaving bag and looked in it. There was some crepe hair, which looks like human hair, but made from wool. Pro knew it was used to make hairpieces. She looked at the bottle of amber liquid, and the label read: Spirit Gum.

"Misdirection!" she bellowed with a vehemence that surprised even her. She turned and ran down the stairs, then went over the stage and stopped herself. She took a couple of deep breaths and then walked through the curtain.

The audience had remained in their seats, but it was obvious they were not happy about it. Two more police cars had pulled up outside, and several more uniformed men and women were there.

Carson was letting people move one at a time from the theater to the lobby. There several officers asked for ID and took the person's information.

Pro approached Tom and said, "I need to question one of the audience members. Can you and an officer bring him onto the stage?"

Chu frowned. "Which one?"

"Tall, older guy with the beard," Pro murmured.

"Okay, we'll bring him right up," Chu told her.

Pro went back behind the curtain and pulled out her phone. Using it as a flashlight, she stumbled around until she found a pair of light switches. She turned them on and florescent work lights popped on.

She found three folding chairs backstage and put them all in the center of the stage facing each other. She finished just as Chu came through the curtain. The man with the beard was right behind him, and a uniformed officer took up the rear.

"Thank you, officer," Pro said, and directed the man to sit in one of the chairs.

The patrolman gave a nod and went back into the audience.

"You're not going to pull my beard again, are you?" the man asked with a slight smile as Pro sat in the chair opposite him.

Chu sat in the third chair, unsure where this was going.

"Well, I might. But it wouldn't be 'again' in your case. Because you're not the same man."

"I don't know what you're talking about, young woman," the man said.

"When I pulled the man's beard, I looked into his eyes. His brown eyes. But when I saw you after Adrianna went on, your eyes were blue, like they are right now." Pro stood. "So, either you pull off the beard, or I will, Max!"

The man looked from Chu to Pro, then with a sigh reached up and gently pulled off the fake beard.

"What the hell—" was all Chu could manage.

Pro went on. "You said it yourself, Max. Look for the misdirection. You sent that guy in the audience to distract me so that I would confront him. But once the show started, he slipped out, and you took his place. You had to watch your little blood trick from out front, didn't you, Max?"

Max pulled the fedora off his head, and he put the beard and the heavy glasses into it. He then plucked off the fake bushy eyebrows. "Yeah, I didn't know it would look that good, Pro."

He reached into his mouth and pulled a set of false fronts off his teeth, and then lastly he peeled off the rubber nose.

"You changed in the room right next to Brent. Did he even know you were there?"

"I don't think so," Max explained, pulling scraps of solidified rubber from his face. "But it gave me a chance to find out who the murderer really is. Did you figure it out from the emails?"

"No. And if the murderer was someone other than Brent, why did you do the sign at Shaut's place and the blood trick here?"

"I didn't say Brent wasn't a killer. But by now you've seen the forensics. They must have told you there were two killers."

"How could you know that?" Chu demanded.

"I knew because I saw the ligature marks around Al's neck. Then I saw the way Louie Tanner had looked, and I could see the differences. It was obvious it was two separate killers. So I set a trap, and the killer took the bait."

Max rose, as did Pro and Chu.

"What are you doing?" Pro snapped.

"If we go out front, I can solve this case for you right now!"

"So can I," Chu said. "You killed Mike Mystique and possibly Brent Williams."

"Come now, detective. I can not only prove who the murderer is, I can give him to you on a plate right now."

"Only if you promise to surrender and come along with us willingly, no tricks!" Pro rasped.

"Pumpkin—"

"Don't call me that," she snapped.

"Once done here, you can lock me in a cell and throw away the key. I needed the time out in the world to find the actual killer. Now I have no problem with incarceration because I can prove my innocence."

"Then let's go," Pro said.

"But no tricks, Max," Chu warned.

"Only the ones I need, detective. Only the ones I need."

21. Metamorphosis

- -

M ax put the hat on the chair and pulled off the coat to leave it covering his disguises.

Pro went out through the curtain first, followed by Max and finally Chu. They all stood on the stage in front of the curtain.

"Ladies and gentlemen," Max announced, his voice filling the small theater, reflecting his training in stagecraft. "You have been more than an audience to a show! You are all witnesses to a crime!"

The crowd murmured and Sergeant Carson ran up the aisle to Pro. "What is this about? Who's this guy?"

"We're about to find out," Pro said.

"Yes," Malcolm Shaut yelled, no slouch in vocal projection either. "We know you killed three people! And tonight you scared Brent into hanging himself."

"That is the way it looks, but I can tell you the truth," Max announced. He went down the stairs and paced in front of the first row.

"This better be good," Pro warned in an undertone.

Max continued. "This all started because I built an illusion, a magic trick called Prism."

An audience member stood. "Hey, you're Max Marvell. I saw you do that trick in Las Vegas."

Max gave a small nod of acknowledgment and went on. "Someone was attempting to copy my effect, to steal an illusion I had worked on for years. I heard of this and communicated with buyers to warn them not to purchase the effect. One man, Albert Floss, was trying to sell it to Malcolm Shaut."

Shaut held up his hands defensively. "I was willing to pay the price, and I wanted to learn the effect. You had no right to keep other magicians from using an illusion."

"I admit my interest was to protect the integrity of the illusion. I came to New York and went to visit Mister Floss, whom I found murdered."

"But you haven't told us why!" another audience member shouted.

"He died because he tried to cheat the man who actually had designed the plans and explanation of my trick — Brent Williams."

"How can you prove that?" Chu demanded from the stage. "Williams is dead!"

"I already proved it when I used the working prototype of Prism down in the workshop of Mister Shaut. The reason I went there was to find the plans. Instead, I found a prototype. And even though

Mister Shaut claims he did it, the workmanship had to be done by Williams."

"Mere conjecture," Shaut pointed out, a bit flushed.

"It is also my conjecture that Floss wanted to cut out Williams and keep the money for the plans for himself. Williams, in a fury, grabbed a display rope off the counter and choked the old man to death. I know this because there was a space on the dusty glass counter where the rope sat." Max looked over at Chu. "You will see the dusty outline in the crime scene photos and you will find the murder weapon at Brent Williams' apartment on 14th Street."

"How do we know you didn't plant it there?" Chu said.

"Because I didn't have it when the police arrested me shortly after Mister Floss was killed. But let us move on, as it is here that it becomes more diabolical."

Carson turned to a lady at the end of an aisle. "You can go to the lobby and give your name and address if you want to leave."

"Are you kidding?" the woman said. "I wouldn't miss this for the world."

"Williams needed a new middleman, because the buyer, Malcolm Shaut, would be furious if he discovered his own assistant had the plans the entire time. So, Williams approached Louie Tanner and Sam Lovell."

"All right, all right," Lovell responded. "Brent asked me, but I turned 'im right down."

"Really?" Max replied.

"I saw it as a problem that I didn't need. And, Max, I tol' you that when you came by me place and dropped off those papers, your wallet, and phone."

The smile on Max's face was broad.

""Wait a minute," Pro protested. "You gave me the box, but his wallet wasn't in it. We found his wallet in the room Mike Mystique was killed."

"I-I misspoke," Lovell gulped, and took a step back. "I meant the things from inside 'is wallet."

"And that's how you fell into my trap, Sam!" Max said. "I dropped off my wallet, but I coated it with a powder that lasts up to seventy-two hours."

Sam Lovell looked at his hands and held them up. "Nothing there."

In one slick move, Max pulled a small black light out of his jacket and turned it on. The move was so bold that Pro, Chu, and Carson all pulled their service weapons and pointed them at Max.

But their eyes immediately went over to Lovell's hands, which glowed with a purplish light.

Max went on. "You saw a chance to remove a competitor, and a disgruntled former lover, as well as get the plans for yourself."

"No, I didn't," Sam denied.

"It all came to me when I saw Louie Tanner dead, and from the marks I knew that a left-handed man had strangled him. Not the right-handed man who killed Floss. That was when I visited you and give you my belongings. I had a hunch you would leave my wallet at a crime scene, but I did not know you would kill your ex-lover, Mike Mystique."

"This is all bull," Lovell said, and moved over toward Sergeant Carson. "Powder on my 'ands or no powder. You can't prove this."

Max held up his hands, and slowly, with a look to Pro, he withdrew a small digital recorder from his pocket.

"You are right. I couldn't prove it. Which is why I had to get here and put a listening device in Brent's dressing room."

He clicked the switch, and the recorder came to life. It was Lovell's voice. "Look I 'ave the plans now, so we'll make the deal and get the money."

Brent's voice filled the air. "But you killed Tanner and Mystique. There was no reason to—"

"You'll do as I say or the same thing will 'appen to you."

Max clicked the button. "Shall I play the part where you came to Brent after his show, strangled him, and hung him up? Come now, once they analyze the writing on the mirror, they will see that a left-handed man wrote it."

In a fast move, Lovell pulled the gun from Carson's holster and held it up to the man's head.

"It don't matter. I wanted to be rid of Tanner and Mystique, but I have the plans and I can go anywhere in the world and sell them. Now everyone step away or the cop gets it."

Lovell backed his way up the stairs with a look of triumph in his eyes.

As he headed up the aisle, a leg jutted out and tripped him.

As Lovell stumbled, a large, bald black man rose from his seat like a phoenix and fell hard upon him, pinning him to the ground. He used his powerful arms to hold the hand with the pistol against the stairs.

Pro gasped. It was Luther!

Instantly, uniformed officers descended upon the fallen criminal, disarmed him, and cuffed him as they pulled him to his feet.

Pro ran up the stairs to Luther. "Omigod! Are you all right?"

"Fine," Luther said with a grin. "Hope it was okay that I stepped in."

"You were amazing," Pro said in awe. Chu was suddenly by her side, and she needed to focus on business.

"Sergeant," Pro said. "I need to arrange transport for two prisoners."

Carson was still angry that his weapon had been confiscated by Lovell. "Yes, ma'am. But don't think we are letting the charge of assault upon a police officer go."

"I fully expect you to file charges," Pro said. "Tom could you please handcuff our other prisoner?"

Chu gave a nod and walked back to Max, who turned around so Chu could fit the restraints on his wrists. A person stood up and clapped. slowly at first.

Then another person got up...and another. Soon, the entire audience was on their feet and applauded as the police escorted Lovell and Max to a waiting car.

22. Ambitious Card

T he next morning, Max woke up in a cell at Midtown North Precinct. He stretched and yawned, wishing there was a way he could conjure a bit of coffee.

He'd spent the evening going over and over his story and why he'd become suspicious of Lovell from the email message about being "one ahead of TM."

He explained it was what clued him, because the words "one ahead" meant that the initials were the previous letters of the alphabet, SL. He'd also been aware that Sam was an interested buyer, but he became the new middleman. Max also explained to Pro that he believed Williams had given Lovell the plans in case anyone searched his apartment.

Max had an idea where they could be.

"So how did this 'bug' in Brent's dressing room work?" demanded Chu.

"It's wireless, self-contained, and used a special radio frequency, which went directly to the recorder. I set it up to turn on and start recording the moment anyone made a sound in the room."

"Pretty neat," Chu admitted.

"Sorry I couldn't help Brent," Max explained. "But, although the listening device recorded Lovell killing him, I didn't know until I listened to it during the intermission, and by then it was too late."

Pro frowned. "You could have warned us it might happen."

"I honestly didn't think Lovell would go that far."

By midnight, the tired Pro and Chu finally had Max taken to a cell with the promise from the magician that he wouldn't pick the lock. Despite that assurance, Pro had his shoes confiscated in case that was where he kept his picks.

However, Max made no trouble. He just lay in bed and caught some shuteye.

Bright and early on Tuesday morning, Pro was getting up at her mother's apartment where she'd spent the night. She had gone directly to Elisha's, so she could tell her mother that Max was safe and in custody.

Pro woke facing the fact that she had to go down to the precinct and resign.

They had caught the killer, and she didn't want to give up her career, but there was no way anyone would excuse Max's escape. Her taking the blame would save the others from losing their jobs.

After showering and dressing, Pro joined her mother for a cup of coffee. Elisha was watching some morning news show, and Pro really was not in the mood.

"Momma, do you have to have that thing blaring?"

"Honey, I like to stay informed…"

"I know, it's just that—"

All at once, the footage from Max's escape was on the television, and Pro sighed. "Not again."

But the image shrank into a small box at the bottom of the screen, and a female reporter was speaking to Mayor Jonas DeMayo.

"So, Your Honor, there has been a lot of controversy about this footage of a man escaping from a holding cell in the Midtown North Precinct late last week."

"Yes, Carole," the mayor said, showing his million-dollar smile. "And as many of you know, that escapee was none other than famed magician Max Marvell, who is also a personal friend."

"There has been a lot of speculation about that over the weekend," Carole said, with an eye to the camera.

"What hasn't been told is that this was a test, requested by myself and our police commissioner," the mayor said, all polished sincerity. "We wanted to make a series of training videos to expose the techniques used by criminals to escape custody. I was lucky that Max was in town and willing to be our 'go-to-guy' for this, the first in a series of daring escapes we can use to train our officers."

"So the officers were aware this was happening?" Carole asked.

"No, this was totally on a need-to-know basis," Mayor DeMayo said. "But it gave us a tremendous teaching tool we can use for years to come."

"Thank you, Your Honor, for coming by today to explain," Carole said and faced the camera. "So there you have it. Max Marvell's daring escape was a planned—"

Elisha clicked off the television. "You think that's what really happened?"

Pro was still catching her breath. A smile came across her face. "Not for a second, but it means I don't have to quit!"

Elisha smiled. "I'm so glad, honey. And you solved the murder?"

"All except where the plans are. Momma, I gotta go see Max. And for once, I know where he is.""

All but running to the subway, Pro was at the precinct in twenty minutes. She headed for the holding cells and there was Sergeant Palos.

"He ain't there, Pro. Mayor called and told us to release him," Palos said. "I gotta ask, were you in on the test, or did they keep you in the dark as well?"

"It surprised me as well," Pro replied. "I'll see if I can track Max down."

She headed into the bullpen, and there was Max sipping on a coffee in the chair next to her desk. He gave a salute with the cardboard cup. "Hey there! Did you hear the news?"

Pro drew close and looked around to make sure no one was listening. "How did you arrange that?"

"I called Jonas yesterday before I met you at the theater. I told him how much a training video would help, and that it was a great way to turn the adverse publicity into good publicity. After all, he is a politician."

"Max, I could kiss you," Pro said.

Max took a sip from his cup. "Good, I'm making progress. So, have you received a warrant for Sam Lovell's shop?"

"It's in the works. What's the rush?"

"Because I want to show you where the plans are. And if they are in police custody as evidence, I don't have to worry about anyone stealing my trick."

Pro sat in her chair. "Is that all that matters to you?"

"No, but it is a consideration. My first concern was the fact that you were ready to resign because of my escape."

"How did you know that?"

Max sipped his coffee enigmatically.

Pro sighed. "I guess you won't tell me."

"I wanted to make sure that I handled the situation," Max said. "You're a good detective, and I wouldn't want you to lose your job over me.""

At that moment, Tom Chu walked into the bullpen and took one look at Max and then stared at Pro. "Did he escape again?"

Pro smiled. "No, it turns out that his escape was an approved training exercise."

This made Tom's eyebrows go up. "Oh, really?"

"That's the official story," Pro explained. "I saw the mayor talk about it on the news this morning."

"Talk about a magic trick." Chu grinned.

"I was just asking Pro about the warrant for Lovell's store," Max said.

"It just came through. I picked up the paperwork on my way up."

Max got up. "Then shall we solve the last part of the mystery? In fact, it might be the most interesting part."

"We were going to go in later with forensics," Chu said.

"I'll wear gloves. Don't you want to know where a magician hides things?"

Chu looked at Pro, sighed wearily, and then said, "Okay, but you're riding in the back, Max."

Soon, they had driven up to the Ansonia Hotel. Max, surprisingly, was quiet throughout the trip. They walked into the massive building and headed for the office marked "Ansonia Realty."

In the small room, Cathy Edmonds rose as the trio entered.

"I can't believe Mister Lovell was arrested," Cathy lamented. "I mean, he was so nice."

Max stepped forward. "Come with us and you can see what he was up to."

Chu raised a hand. "Wait a moment, Max. We don't want too many people. It might corrupt the evidence chain."

"I think she has a right to find out what Mister Lovell was doing," Max said.

"I can stand outside, if that's what you need."

"I brought an extra pair of gloves," offered Max.

Cathy grabbed a large key ring, and the quartet moved down the hall toward Lovell's shop.

Max went on. "I found out that Sam was interested in the history of the Ansonia. Isn't that right, Cathy?"

"Hm? Oh yeah, he was always looking at the blueprints and stuff. He told me he was a history buff."

"Actually, I did some digging into the history of the hotel myself to find out what had piqued his interest. My results surprised me."

They had reached the door to Lovell's shop, and Cathy looked at her keys to select the correct one. As she did, Max, Pro, and Chu pulled out latex gloves and put them on.

"So what did you find, Max?" Pro said.

"Didn't I teach you anything, pumpkin?" Max smirked. "Show, don't tell."

The door opened and Max handed a pair of gloves to the baffled Cathy, as Chu murmured to Pro, "He called you 'pumpkin,' and you let him get away with it."

"He also saved me from resigning and either of us from being in trouble," Pro agreed. "I'll let him enjoy himself this once."

Max hit the light switch with his gloved hand. "The city has many strange stories, but one of them is that the mail used to be shot around the city at thirty miles per hour in pneumatic tubes."

"Really?" Cathy said. "That's amazing."

Pro and Tom exchanged a glance.

Max led them through the curtain and to the back room.

"But also amazing was that the Ansonia was part of that route. The hotel had pneumatic tubes running throughout the building, for not only mail, but for communication from guests to staff."

There were shelves of props in the back room on standing units, all carefully marked. Max walked over to the one empty wall and knocked on it as the others watched. He came to a place where the sound was remarkably hollow.

"Ah, and I think we have it," Max said as he tapped up and down and studied the wall. At last he put his hands on it and pressed so that a part of the wall sprung open on a hidden hinge.

"Hey, that's not supposed to do that," Cathy said, annoyed.

"That's all right," Max stated as he peeked behind the moving panel. He opened the door wide, and you could see the brick of the original wall, and in front of it, three large tubes. The pipes each had a metal fitting over the end. Max tried them one at a time, and on the third one, it turned easily in his hand. "I believe we have found what we are looking for."

He untwisted the metal cap and lifted it off. Then, he took his first two gloved fingers, shoved them into the pipe, and was obviously feeling around.

Finally, with a triumphant look on his face, he pulled several rolled-up sheets of paper from the tube.

"Well, I never," Cathy exclaimed.

The paper tube was at least three feet long, and Max knelt to the floor to unroll it.

There were several pages of complicated sketches of the two prisms. The paper had mathematical calculations with careful instructions.

Max rolled it back up and offered it to Pro, who took the papers.

She shook her head. "So for these, four people died."

"That and the fifty-thousand Shaut wanted to pay for it," Max said. "So, shall I escort you back to your office, Mrs. Edmonds?"

"It's actually Miss Edmonds, or Ms."

"Really, how delightful," Max said as he put out his arm and the blonde took it. They headed out of the room. "I understand you like magic?"

"I love it! Do you know any tricks?"

"Quite a few, quite a few," Max boasted as they walked.

Pro watched them go, her mouth a tight line.

"Relax, Pro," Chu said. "I thought you didn't want him seeing your mother."

"I don't, but I don't like him playing games."

"I'll call forensics, and we'll have this place photographed and categorized. There's a lot here," Chu observed.

An hour later, with the plans still in hand, Chu turned over the investigation to the forensic team. They headed back to the realty office to find Max still entertaining Miss Edmonds with a series of illusions that he pulled from his pocket.

"That really isn't my card," Cathy was saying, as Max held a five of diamonds.

"Really?" Max replied. He rubbed the card against his sleeve and turned it over. It was now the jack of clubs.

"That's it! How did you do that?" she gushed.

"Just a little magic," Max suggested, then looked at the two detectives. "Are you two done?"

"Yes, we're leaving," Pro said. "Miss Edmonds, the forensic team will let you know when you can lock up."

"Great," she said, then turned back to Max and held out her card. "I get done at 5:00. My number's on the card. I wrote my private number on the back."

"Thank you," Max said and kissed her hand gallantly.

"Oh, a gentleman," she cooed.

"Max!" Pro hissed, catching what he'd done.

"I'll tell her," the magician said. "And for being such an excellent audience, here is a lovely ring."

"Oh?" she said, amused. Then she looked carefully at the bauble and her own finger. "Hey that was my ring! How did you do that?"

Max gave a wave and headed out the door. Pro and Max were behind him. "Well, I am going to pick up my luggage from Adrianna and move back into the Waldorf, if you have no objections."

"Why the hurry?" Pro stated snidely. "Got a date tonight?"

"Actually, I do," Max beamed.

""With Miss Hot Pants in there?" Pro grumbled.

"No, dear, with your mother," Max said breezily. "Why would I want a confection when a real woman is available, pumpkin?"

He walked away as Pro and Chu approached their car.

"And don't call me pumpkin," Pro shouted after him.

23. Scotch And Soda

T wo weeks later, Pro sat across from Luther at a lovely outdoor restaurant on Amsterdam Avenue on a gorgeous night. They both had frozen drinks in front of them and were very relaxed.

She stared into his eyes. "You've been very patient."

"Well, I understand your work. I mean, my hours are steady, but you get called out all the time."

"That date at the movies—"

Luther pointed at her. "I did finally get to kiss you."

"Yeah, and then I had to run off to a crime scene and leave you there."

"I tol' you that was all right."

"Then last week, our walk in the park." Pro smiled. "That was romantic—"

"Until I had to cover someone's shift last minute," Luther shrugged, as he took her hand and brought it to his lips.

Pro shivered and looked at Luther through half-closed eyes.

"Pro?" a voice said nearby.

Pro pulled her hand free and turned to see Max walk over.

"Hey," Luther said, "you're that guy from the theater."

"Yes! You were the man who stopped Lovell from getting away." Max held out his hand and Luther shook it.

"Has anyone ever told you that you look like that guy from Vegas?"

"You mean Max Marvell?"

"Yeah, that's the guy," Luther said.

"That's who I am!" Max announced.

"Really?" Luther beamed. "I saw that TV special you did ten years ago—"

The two men talked, and Max pulled a chair over to their table and did a coin routine. The pair of them became engrossed and ignored Pro completely.

Pro sipped her drink, growing more annoyed with each passing minute. Finally she said, "Uh, Max, we're on a date."

"This will only take a minute," Max said.

"Yeah, do that again," Luther said, caught up in Max's trick.

Pro stood and headed inside to the ladies' room. She pulled out her phone and called her mother.

"Yes, sweetie," Elisha answered.

"Max is doing tricks for my date!" Pro raged.

"That's nice, dear."

"I thought you two were spending time together! Can't you keep him busy?"

"Honey, we are taking it slow. I believe that was your advice."

"But, Mom," Pro snapped, and then lowered her voice. "Tonight's the night!"

"What night?"

Pro wanted to smash her phone. "Are you thick? The night. The first night! Luther and me doing — y'know."

"Oh, honey, that's wonderful."

"No, it's not. Max is ruining it!"

"Well, what do you want me to do?" Elisha replied.

"Call him! Invite him over, get him out of my hair."

"You told me I should take it slow," Elisha chided.

"Well, I have taken it too slow, and he's interfering! Call him, tell him you have to see him. I don't know, tell him your loins ache for him."

This made Elisha burst out in laughter. "He wouldn't expect that."

"Just please do something."

"All right, sugar, I got this," Elisha said and ended the call.

Pro took a steadying breath and returned to the table where Max was starting another routine. All at once, Max's phone rang.

"Pardon me," he said to Luther and held the phone to his ear. "What is it, Elisha?"

Pro watched as her father's face turned very red and his breathing quickened.

"Ache, huh?" Max said, his mouth dry. "I'll... um... be right over." He stood. "I gotta go. Nice meeting you, Luther."

Max walked away briskly.

"Wow! You know that guy?" Luther said excitedly.

"Actually, he's my father."

"Really? He is amazing. He can do great things with his hands."

Pro picked up her margarita, which was a little less frozen, and took a sip. She spoke in a sultry voice, "I was wondering if you were good with your hands."

Luther suddenly had a look similar to Max's a few moments ago.

"I'd like to think I am," Luther gulped.

"Tell you what, let's go to your place, and I'll show you what tricks I know," she offered with the sexiest wink she could muster.

Luther's smile was a beautiful thing to see.

The End

About The Author

Halfway through college I experienced an identity crisis, joined the army and ended up stationed in Frankfurt, Germany.

One night in 1979, I was in a club where a beautiful girl in a silver costume belly danced through the room. I approached her and begged to take classes with her.

Over the next ten years, I started start my own business. My performing life grew to include cruise ships, night clubs, resorts in the Poconos and Catskills, and TV appearances.

In 1990, I auditioned at the Taj Mahal in Atlantic City and spent two years performing with the Taj Players. It was there I met my husband, Arjay Lewis. As our lives grew together, I began transitioning into teaching the dance, and found a fulfillment I never expected.

My husband has always been a writer, and when he started publishing, I became inspired to try my hand at the romantic mystery genre. This was a perfect complement to Arjay's paranormal mysteries.

Today we truly are, partners in crime…fiction

Books from Mindbender Press

Paranormal Mystery
Fire In The Mind
Seduction In The Mind
Reunion In The Mind
Haunted In The Mind
Devotion In The Mind
Asylum In The Mind
Specter In The Mind
Vengeance In The Mind
Echoes In The Mind
Infection In The Mind
Justice In The Mind
Ritual In The Mind
Vengeance In The Mind
Echoes In The Mind
Justice In The Mind
Ritual In The Mind
Vanished In The Mind

Horror
The Muse
Kept In The Dark
The Vanishing
Digger

Romantic Suspense
A Study In Murder
Murder By Misdirection
Vanishing Act

NYPD Wizard Detective
The Wizards Of Central Park West
The Vampires Of Greenwich Village
The Werewolves Of Washington Square

Free Prequel

A street magician is murdered, a knife sticking from his chest. Can a NYPD rookie use her unique talents to find a killer?

Prophecy "Pro" Thompson is a female African-American, NYPD uniformed officer. Pro and her partner find a street performer stabbed through the heart and Pro decides to work the case in her free time.

During her investigation, Pro meets magician Jamie Tobin, a charming Irishman who tries to amaze her but becomes more interested in romancing her.

If you enjoy a kick-ass female protagonist, and a story mixed with crime, romance and comedy, you will love this fast-paced novella by Debra Snow.

This prequel takes places before *Murder By Misdirection*. Find out how the story begins!

http://www.debrasnow.com